Praise for Heather Blanton

"Heather Blanton is blessed with a natural storytelling ability, an 'old soul' wisdom, and wide expansive heart. Her characters are vividly drawn, and in the Western settings where life can be hard, over quickly, and seemingly without meaning, she reveals Larger Hands holding everyone and everything together."

— MARK RICHARD, EXECUTIVE PRODUCER OF AMC'S *HELL ON WHEELS*

"Fans of Louis L'Amour and Francine Rivers will find Blanton's stories even more enthralling. With wit, a clear author's voice, and storytelling chops that rival the best— you'll have found your new favorite storyteller!"

— CARRIE FANCETT PAGELS, AWARD- WINNING AUTHOR

"Masterful at gritty fiction that points to the ultimate Creator, Heather will become one of your favorite Christian fiction authors."

— KARI TRUMBO, *USA TODAY* BESTSELLING AUTHOR

GRACE BE A LADY

GRACE BE A LADY

❦

HEATHER BLANTON

✝

Grace Be a Lady
Paperback Edition
Copyright © 2024 (As Revised) by Heather Blanton

CKN Christian Publishing
An Imprint of Wolfpack Publishing
1707 E. Diana Street
Tampa, FL 33610

www.cknchristianpublishing.com

Grace Be a Lady was originally self-published in 2015 by Heather Blanton.

Scripture taken from: *The Holy Bible, King James Version*. Cambridge Edition: 1769; *King James Bible Online*, 2024. www.kingjames-bibleonline.org. Public Domain.

Paperback ISBN 978-1-63977-476-0
Ebook ISBN 978-1-63977-475-3

Author's Note

Dear Readers,

Thank you so very much for giving *Grace be a Lady* a chance. While I've salted my previous books with dashes of history, this book is different. I've taken an actual historical event and woven a fictional thread in with it. My years of research into the Johnson County Range War revealed stunning passion and amazing cruelty. The things men will do, all the ways they will sell their souls for the fleeting taste of power and money is, an infuriating hallmark of our species. At times in this story, you won't be able to tell the truth from the fiction as the truth is so incredibly startling.

A big thanks and a kiss to my husband for his unwavering support. A rough-talking, hardworking, blue-collar guy, he is kind enough to bust his backside so that I can sit on my ever-widening one and write my stories. He just hopes, one day, I'll make enough money to buy him a private helicopter. It could happen. With God, all things are possible.

I would be incredibly remiss if I didn't thank the team that makes my novels possible. This is far from a one-man show. I have editors, beta readers, cover designers, and friends who offer their expertise, opinions, and advice. God has truly blessed me with an amazing support network. So, thank you to Kim Huther, Vicki Prather, Heather Baker, Terri Sullivan, Lisa Janey, Jean Stewart, Carole Sanders, and Carol Gehringer!

Finally, and most importantly, I thank my Lord and Savior for blessing me exceedingly and abundantly. Not to mention what He did on the cross. I am overwhelmed by his love and compassion every moment!

I hope at the end of this book, you'll be sad it's over. *That* is what makes a novel great, the way characters linger around the edges of your heart for days, if not forever. I've given it my best shot to make this a story you won't soon forget. So, happy reading, and God bless!

Heather

For now, we see through a glass, darkly, but then face to face:

Now, I know in part, but then shall I know even as also I am known.

— 1 CORINTHIANS 13:12 KJV

Preface

Every family has a legend or two. These old, familiar stories, told with smiles and winks at family reunions and holiday gatherings, are often grounded in *some* facts. Over the generations, though, the truth and the lies tend to merge, intertwining like mist and smoke.

This is the story of my great-great-grandmother, as it was related to me one snowy Christmas in Wyoming.

If it's not true, it oughta be.

GRACE BE A LADY

Prologue

❧

"**M**iss?" Brittle questioned gently as he tapped on the changing room door. No response. Oh, she was a strange one. What girl wanted to try on her brother's clothes to make sure they'd fit him? She was probably a suffocating mother hen.

He tapped again and listened. He couldn't detect any sound coming from the other side, no rustle of dungarees, no soft whisper of cotton. "Miss, is everything all right?"

Greeted again with silence, he frowned, debated, and then pulled his key ring from his pocket.

"Brittle, I don't have all day," a shaggy cowboy hollered from the counter. "The boys are waitin' on me."

Brittle slid the key into the lock. "One moment, this won't take long." He pushed the door open ever so slowly, just in case the poor girl had a hearing problem or something of the like. Yet, the more the door opened, the more he realized the closet was empty. He saw the scissors she had asked for sitting on the bench. And then he spied a neatly folded stack of money sitting beside them. He stepped in, picked up the bills, and counted—more than enough by one whole dollar. The young lady was gone, as were the new clothes, but she had paid. A strange deal, but a square one.

"Brittle," the man called again, fuming.

Brittle walked back to the counter, his active imagination creating an injured brother who had been hiding in the woods, perhaps shot in a botched bank robbery. His sister had come in for new clothes. And maybe she and her outlaw brother were on their way to Hole-in-the-Wall. Maybe there was no brother. Perhaps Etta Place had come in his store to buy clothes for Butch Cassidy himself!

His mind flustered with thoughts of gunfighters, bank robberies, and determined posses, he finished up with the scowling customer. Then, with a wistful sigh, Brittle folded his arms and leaned on the counter. Longing for some excitement, he grudgingly acknowledged that Misery, Wyoming, was, in truth, about the most boring place on earth.

Chapter One

❧❧❧

"**G**race, you are too beautiful and gentle to be trapped in a loveless marriage with a man like Bull Hendrick."

Alone with her photographer in the parlor, Grace allowed Seth Lattimore to slip his hand on top of hers. She should have stood up or at least slid further down the settee, but the young artist's eager green eyes held her perfectly still. Like a flower in need of water, her heart had thirstily drunk in Seth's rain of compliments and flirtatious remarks. Their hours together, as she posed for his portraits, had left them too much time to talk, to move toward one another.

"*I* would treat you like a princess," he whispered, grasping her hand. "*I* would never raise my hand to you...and I swear *I* would never cheat on you."

Grace felt herself give in a little. Seth pulled her hand to his cheek and held it there as if it were the hand of a queen, the queen he cherished.

In six years, Harry *Bull* Hendrick hadn't touched

3

her with such reverence or affection, not once. Nor had he said a kind word to her. The very moment they'd married, he'd changed into a monster. He'd gone from gently wooing her in fancy restaurants to lording over her like a slave owner, the change as sudden and severe as the outbreak of a summer thunderstorm.

He bellowed, grabbed, shoved, controlled.

Seth, with his smoldering jade eyes and boyish grin, was kind, supportive, and dangerously sympathetic. The perfect temptation. Now, Grace sat squarely in a moment from which she should run.

You're not happy in your marriage, a voice whispered. *Bull hasn't been faithful...*

The warmth of Seth's hand on her cheek and the reverent way he touched her shoulder could almost make her weep. He moved closer and Grace closed her eyes. She felt so empty and dry.

Just one drop of water...

Just one kiss...

The doors to the parlor burst open. Bull exploded into the room like a thunderbolt. Gasping in terror, Grace and Seth leaped to their feet. Her husband, a huge man with seething, dark eyes and shoulders nearly as broad as the doorway, whipped a revolver from beneath his jacket and pointed it at Seth. Grace looked into the darkness of the barrel and her heart froze.

"Your services are no longer required here, Mr. Lattimore," Bull spoke calmly, but she knew his tone belied a maelstrom of fury. He cocked the hammer and the sound was deafening. "Not here. Not anywhere in Chicago."

"M—Mr. Hendrick," Seth pleaded, his hands rising in surrender. "You've got this all wrong. We weren't doing anything, merely talking."

Bull fired above Seth's head, the bullet shattering a gas lamp on the wall. Grace screamed and covered her ears. She wondered if Seth understood his life was hanging by a fraying thread.

"I said your services are no longer required."

Her photographer got the picture. He shot Grace a look of regret so brief she nearly missed it and then scrambled out the door, stumbling over an ottoman as he fled. The parlor was full of his equipment. Somehow, she doubted he would be back for it.

Fighting a rising sense of dread and desperation, Grace lowered her hands, forcing herself to straighten up and stop looking as if she was waiting for a slap across the face. Defiant, she met Bull's gaze as he swung the gun over to her.

"Well, well, the missus has been found out."

He cocked the hammer again.

She should have been afraid but, instead, saw the weapon as a possible escape. All these years of living with a man who would rather beat her than offer a kind word had turned her soul into a desert of bitterness. If not for the wonderful gift of their son, Grace was sure she wouldn't have survived Bull's cruelty.

But she had to want to live. If she was gone, that would mean Bull would raise Hardy alone. The thought of her child growing up to be like this greedy, belligerent, short-tempered tyrant incensed her. "We weren't doing anything." She curled her hands into fists. "Your imagination is running away with you."

Bull smiled, a soulless expression that reminded Grace of a shark, and released the hammer on his gun. He shoved the piece back into the holster beneath his coat, his dark eyes glittering. "Lonnie, boy," he called over his shoulder. "Come in here. My wife thinks me stupid, or blind...or both."

Lonnie, Bull's malicious but loyal sidekick-henchman, strolled into the room. Leering triumphantly at Grace, he pulled a notebook from his pocket. Oh, this was the little limey's moment indeed, Grace realized. He'd made advances to her over and over these last few years, and she had rejected him outright, twice with a stinging slap. A stumpy bloke with the hygiene of a dock-worker, she'd been plain about her disgust. Now, the smirk on his face said he would relish this moment of her destruction.

Swallowing to fight a dry mouth, Grace kept her face perfectly still, perfectly blank. Lonnie flipped through the notebook, found something interesting, and started reading. "Mr. Lattimore: You are looking particularly lovely today, Mrs. 'Endrick. I pray you 'ad sweet dreams. Perhaps even abou' us?" His limey accent, indicative of his rough background, added a tawdry layer to his quotes, one he willingly played up. "Mrs. 'Endrick: You cross my mind quite frequently, Mr. Lattimore, often at the most inappropriate times."

Shame heated Grace's cheeks. Bull's lips tightened. Lonnie flipped to a new page, scanned the passage silently, leered at Grace for an instant, and then went back to the page to perform again. "I observed Mr. Lattimore approaching Mrs. 'Endrick in the study. 'e began to re-arrange her curls on her shoulder. Moving in very closely, they whispered to each other, but I could not discern their words. 'Owever, Mr. Lattimore brushed his mouth across Mrs. 'Endrick's forehead and then proceeded to pull the pins from her hair—"

"That's enough," Grace snapped. She speared Bull with a glare that most likely had no effect on him. "You make my friendship with Mr. Lattimore sound so filthy." But it *had* bordered on inappropriate. She turned away from Bull and Lonnie's victory stares. Truthfully, the border had been crossed, weeks back. Nothing physical had ever happened between her and Seth, but her mind had been filled with him. Bull's groping and gruff advances had pushed her dreams into a realm where a married woman, even one who had been cheated on and beaten repeatedly, should never go.

"You will be leaving us, Grace," Bull said, still using that chillingly-calm voice. "Lonnie will escort you to the train station. Ride to where the ticket takes you."

Grace felt raw panic trying to rise to the surface as Bull walked over and grabbed her arm, spinning her around. "I'm sure you'll find suitable employment there for a woman of your loose morals."

"*My* morals?"

He didn't respond to her indignation. Instead, he swept a black curl off her forehead and dug his fingers deeper into her flesh. "I cannot abide a lying, cheating wife." His fingers sank deeper. Grace tried to twist away from him and hold back a cry. His fury emanated from his beefy hands as they gouged into her flesh. "You and Mr. Lattimore are mighty lucky I'm in a good mood." Finally, she cried out, and he thrust her at Lonnie. "No one makes a fool out of me, Grace. Not without paying a price."

❧❧

Grace sat silent and motionless in the carriage as the vehicle stopped and started, working its way through the congestion of horses and wagons, pedestrians and trolleys. She desperately wanted to sob, scream—pound her fists on something as panic crept in.

She glanced at Lonnie, eyeing her with that ever-present leer, and knew she couldn't give him the satisfaction. Instead, she fluffed her mutton sleeves and attempted to pull together a plan of some sort. She *had* to remain calm and rational if she wanted to have any hope of getting to Hardy. No matter where the ticket was taking her, she could get off early, in Wheaton, perhaps. She'd managed to grab her reticule on the way out and kept it hidden in the folds of her skirt. The purse contained some spending money. Not much, but she could sneak back into Chicago, take Hardy, and then they could seek refuge at Father Benetton's church ...just until she could figure things out.

"Now, luv," Lonnie said, cleaning his nails with his pocketknife. "I'll explain to you 'ow this is going to work. The train ticket in my pocket," he patted his chest, "will take you all the way to Misery, Wyoming."

A twitch in Grace's eyebrow betrayed her reaction to the name.

"Yes, Bull picked the town out just for you, luv. Said he 'oped it delivered. Anyway, you will get off the train there and not before." He snapped the knife shut and leaned forward. "If you don' check in with Misery's lawman, luv, 'Ardy will be shipped off to some boarding school in Paris. Or maybe Rome. Possibly even Timbuktu. Do you take my meaning, luv?"

Grace's heart broke as the threat sank in. Her chin quivered, and the lump in her throat tried to explode into a sob. Completely out of hope, she could do nothing but pray.

She prayed she would dance on Bull's grave one day soon.

Falling back on the loathing that Lonnie so readily evoked in her, Grace raised her chin. "Don't call me *luv*."

Chapter Two

❧

Lulled by the sway and click-clack of the train, Grace stared blankly out the window at the towering, snow-capped mountains in the distance. She ached so much to see Hardy that she felt nauseated, but her bitterness toward Bull kept invading her mind, replacing the ache with hate. Somehow, some way, she would get back to her son and free them of Bull, even if she had to kill the man to do it.

She at least had some measure of peace, knowing he wouldn't hurt their son. And, soon, she would be with Hardy again.

Unfortunately, the plan to make that happen hadn't formed yet.

The train's whistle blew and she snapped back, taking in the handful of weathered, forlorn-looking buildings on the horizon.

Misery.

Not much more than a hamlet, it consisted of

about a dozen buildings sitting on a wide, rolling plain of golden fall grass. In the background, the mammoth Big Horn Mountains grazed the cloudless sky while fingers of evergreen forests struggled toward the town, not quite reaching it. Her stomach fell as she realized the job prospects in such a small community would be limited, to say the least.

Perhaps Bull had known that.

Grace pulled away from the window and laced her fingers over her stomach. Had Bull sent her here, knowing the only way to survive might be to become a...a...?

She couldn't even *think* the word. There was absolutely no way, no circumstance, no situation that would push her in that direction. There had to be some other kind of job in this town. And she would find it.

❧❧❧

Amid the hiss of steam and laughter of warm reunions, Grace climbed down from the train and stepped out onto the platform. Another dozen or so people disembarked as well and filtered past her. She watched them go, so envious that they probably had homes, friends, and loved ones waiting for them. She felt that tightening in her throat again and angrily forced it back. *Focus on the job.*

Grace marched over to a window of the rail office to assess her appearance. Her honey-tinged golden hair was twisted in a stylish chignon atop her head, but the hair-do was precarious at best. Sighing, she re-tucked some stray hairs and fluffed the bun, pinched her cheeks to add some color, and then looked down at her dress. The bodice and skirt, made of sky-blue satin, were trimmed in midnight-blue velvet and draped with generous folds of powder-blue lace. A row of petite velvet bows paraded down the center of her ensemble. She was a tad over-dressed to be searching for a job. Resigned, Grace puffed the sleeves, smoothed the folds of her skirt, and marched toward the town, her fishtail bustle swishing demurely in the dust.

She'd only gone a few steps when she realized the first building on the main street was the sheriff's office. Relieved she wouldn't have to go asking about for directions, she entered the rather small, unpainted clapboard building with as much pride as she could muster, though she felt like she was going to see the principal.

As she stepped into the office, an old man snatched his boots off the desk and attempted to leap to a standing position, but the rickety chair tilted back, and stiff joints caused him to flounder comically for a moment, like an upside-down turtle trying to work its way back to its feet.

He grabbed the edge of the desk to finish pulling himself up, flashing Grace a mouthful of decayed, yellowed teeth, evidently pleased he'd managed to stand. No small victory, as he was a portly man. Every button on his worn plaid shirt strained against its hole. "Yes, ma'am, what can I do for you?" His eyes roved boldly over her.

The light glinted off the star on his chest and her

mouth went slack with amazement. "You're the sheriff?"

He puffed up and pushed a greasy strand of hair behind one ear. "Yes, ma'am. For two years now."

"Well," Grace mumbled, studying the pine floor. *Well, what?* It didn't matter who the sheriff was and he struck her as exactly the kind of man Bull would know in a town like this. *So be it.* She jerked her head up. "My name is Grace Hendrick. Consider me checked in." She twirled on her heel and marched out of the office in a flurry of dusty-blue lace.

Why the heck does Pa keep that worthless shirker around? It just doesn't make sense.

Thad Walker stood in the saloon's doorway, staring through the meager crowd and thin haze of smoke at Trampas Cheever. The ranch foreman was leaning on the bar chatting up a saloon gal instead of doing his job—rounding up horses.

Disgusted, Thad balled his right hand into a fist and, with his left, slowly pushed through the door. One of these days, he would catch Trampas doing something that was, without a doubt, a firing offense —no gray areas—and finally, he'd have his pa's okay to give this lickspittle his last payday. Till then...

"Trampas." The man slid his gaze from the pretty little distraction to Thad. "You were supposed to have that string of ponies ready to go first thing. You should have already been back at the ranch with 'em."

Trampas turned toward the bar and tossed down his whiskey. "I got thirsty."

Thad was in no mood. A hailstorm had knocked down twenty-plus acres of wheat last night. Some of the calves were showing signs of coccidiosis. Six hands had ridden out for the gold fields, and now this cocky piece of trash hadn't even strung the remuda together. The ranch was in desperate need of those fresh horses.

Betty Jean, the sweet little redhead entertaining Trampas, must have seen the thundercloud forming on Thad's face. She swallowed and backed a few feet down the bar.

Striking like a lightning bolt, Thad grabbed Trampas and spun him around. The man's eyebrows shot straight up.

"You don't respect me, that's one thing." Thad stepped in closer. "But not doing your job disrespects my father. You and I are going to have to come to an understanding. Is today the day?"

Trampas stood up to Thad for a second, then smiled and inched back. "No, sir." He grabbed his hat off the bar. "I'll get right to those horses."

A smirk played on the man's lips as he sidestepped Thad with a nod and departed the saloon. Thad grit his teeth, wondering when—not if—a fight was coming. Maybe not today, but Trampas was going to get that smirk knocked right off his bony face, and Thad had the fist that could do it.

Ignoring the stunned silence and transfixed stares of saloon patrons, Thad stomped out onto the boardwalk and paused. To his left, Trampas sauntered off toward the stockyard, long legs moving at a leisurely pace. The ranch hand's gangly frame reminded Thad of a praying mantis.

And he hated bugs.

Feeling more than a little surly, he scanned the street in search of his brother but found something that lifted his mood right considerable. A pretty little strawberry-blonde in a powder-blue dress stood outside the bakery. He watched as she tugged on her shirtwaist, adjusted her fluffy, lacy sleeves, rolled her shoulders, and then stepped inside.

Lot of fuss for some bread.

He couldn't explain why, but he waited a minute for her to come out. When she did, the sagging slope of her shoulders told him things hadn't gone to her liking. She took a few steps with her head down but then seemed to think better of it. She stopped, raised her chin, and marched into the general store.

It didn't take a genius to figure out she was probably hunting for a job. He rubbed his neck and gave serious thought to trying to intersect paths with her. But he didn't really have time. Buddy, at the blacksmith shop, was waiting for him.

He literally wavered as he took a step toward responsibility, and away from her. His weathered cowboy boots wanted to follow those petite lace-up boots, his brain wanted to take care of ranching business. Both his brothers would already be across the street, asking the young lady to join them for ice cream. And that was exactly why *he* was his father's right-hand man...or, at least, used to be.

Besides, Misery was a small town. He would run into her again. He gained enough willpower from that to set off for the blacksmith shop, but not without one last glance back at the general store.

The unpleasant meeting with the sheriff behind her, Grace surveyed the street, wondering where to start. On a pure whim, she marched off to her left and grabbed the first door knob she came to but stopped before she burst through it like some crazy woman. Even though she was dirty and desperately wanted to wash her hair, she noticed a few of the men in town had assessed her with appreciative glances. Thankfully assured she didn't look like the ragamuffin she felt like, she straightened her clothing again, tucked and smoothed her hair, and blew out a hopeful breath.

A bakery, tailor shop, general store, bank, and a men's clothing store—she hit them all in determined succession. The answer was the same at each place: they weren't hiring. The older lady at the bakery did, however, suggest that Grace go to the feed store. That's where, she said, most job openings were posted. Grace appreciated the sympathy in the woman's soft smile and tried to let it buoy her flagging spirits.

She kept her head up and her shoulders squared as she crossed the street on her way to the feed store, but her journey was wearing on her. A train bench didn't make the most comfortable bed, and she hadn't slept well in days. Worse, she'd kept her meals small to stretch her money. Consequently, as the boardwalk angled up a hill, she felt hunger and weakness burn through her core. In another minute, she was light-headed. With relief, Grace spied a bench just outside the feed store and aimed for it. Shaking off some dizziness, she sat down and closed her eyes.

Oh, I can't feel like this, she scolded, rubbing her temple. *No one will hire a weak-kneed daisy on the verge of fainting.*

"Ma'am, are you all right?"

Startled, Grace swung her head up and found herself staring into the broad, handsome face of a smooth-shaven cowboy. Blue eyes, framed at the corners with weathered creases, shimmered with concern. Sprigs of rebellious blonde hair paraded across his worried brow, sneaking out from beneath a white hat. Practically in one motion, he snatched the Stetson off his head, ran his hand through his hair, and sat down beside her.

"You look a little peaked. Is there anything I can do for you, ma'am? You're new to Misery, right?"

New to misery? She could have laughed at the question. No, she was old friends with misery, but he didn't need to hear her problems. Still, that gaze, brimming with compassion, drew her in, made her want to reach out for help.

"Do you know where I can find a job?"

His face fell. "No, ma'am, I'm really sorry, I don't. Even if I did, it'd be ranch work." Then he flashed her a sideways smile as he spun his hat in his hands. "And you're kind of scrawny for a cowhand." The young man had a rather attractive dimple in his cheek, but it disappeared as he turned more serious. "My name is Thad Walker, ma'am." He stuck out his hand. "I'm pleased to meet you."

She accepted the shake but without much enthusiasm. "I'm Grace Hendrick." She didn't have time to be distracted by that dimpled smile or those magical, ice-blue eyes. If he couldn't help her, it was time to move on. She rose to her feet and he joined her. She took an instant to notice the way he towered over her, but the flap and flutter of papers in front of her drew her attention to a board with notices tacked to it.

He chucked a thumb at it. "Those are the job listings. I haven't seen anything, though, that wasn't ranch work, like I said."

She skimmed over the notices. *Ranch hand wanted. Experienced ranch hands wanted. Bunkhouse cook.* Intrigued, Grace stepped closer and stopped that notice from waving in the breeze. "What is a bunkhouse cook?"

Thad placed his hat back on his head and cleared his throat. "Well, for that one, ma'am, you'd have to live in the bunkhouse with all the hands."

She snatched her hand away. "Oh." She continued reading, and with each notice, her spirits fell a degree more.

"Ma'am?" Thad put one hand on his gun and leaned slightly toward Grace, enough to let her know the question was delicate. "I don't mean to pry, but are you, you know, all right? I mean, do you have a place to stay and such?"

"Oh, yes, I'm fine," she said, consciously lifting her face and forcing warmth into her expression. "I have plenty of time to find work."

He studied her, as if debating the truth of the answer.

"Thad!"

His eyes shot past her to a man hailing him.

"Your wagon's ready. Everything's loaded."

Thad sighed and returned to Grace. He seemed to want to say something but, after an awkward silence, tipped his hat. "Good day then, Miss Hendrick. There's not much to Misery. I'm sure we'll run into each other again. At least, I hope so."

Grace nodded but didn't say anything. If Thad Walker couldn't help her find work, he was useless and his flattery worthless. In spite of herself, she watched him walk away. He was handsome, tall, and muscular. His tan corduroys, a bit dirty but in good shape, slid appealingly over powerful legs. In fact, he was well-dressed, and she assumed then that he was a man of means. Perhaps in Misery he might be someone good to know...eventually.

But, for the moment, he wasn't hiring either, which meant she had to keep looking. Grace closed her eyes, took a breath, and went back to the postings one more time. "Please, there has to be something here." *Farrier. Blacksmith apprentice. Ranch hand for a widow lady...*

Her eyes went back to that one. *Ranch hand for a widow lady. Small ranch. Only 100 head and some farm animals. Experience preferred.* Here someone had squeezed in above that *but will train the right man. Contact Raney Lawson at the...*

Grace scrunched up her face. A symbol of some kind finished the sentence. An *R* inside a diamond. *The Diamond R?*

The seed of an idea sprouted.

The man who had hailed Thad Walker walked over

to the bulletin board with a paper in his hand. "Mornin', ma'am."

Grace nodded a greeting as he shifted notes around to make room for a new notice. "Excuse me." She could barely keep the excitement from her voice. "But if I wanted to find Raney Lawson, how would I go about that?"

The man jerked a spare thumb tack from the board and pinned up his note. Some notice about the cattle inspector coming to town. "Well, today's Monday. She usually comes in for supplies around noon." He faced her, twisting his mustache. "But if you miss her, I could draw you a passable map. Her spread's about eight miles west of town on the Crazy Woman."

Grace frowned. The Crazy Woman? But more importantly, eight miles? It might as well be eight hundred. She had no money for a buggy. But she had a plan and intended to see it through. "Thank you. I'll try to catch her at noon."

Ignoring the rumbling in her demanding stomach, Grace hurried back down the street.

Chapter Three

❦

T had snapped the reins and drove the wagon out of the feed store's warehouse. About to pull out onto the street, he searched for Grace, hoping to get one more glimpse of her. No longer sitting on the bench, she was, instead, striding down the boardwalk. Entranced, he paused the horses and watched, taking in the sway of her hips, that tiny waist, bustle swishing back and forth like a hypnotist's watch. Yeah, he could make a habit of this.

Grace Hendrick was just about the prettiest thing Thad had ever seen in his life. From across the street, he had been impressed, but up close, his knees had darn near buckled when she hit him with those eyes. Deep and round, they were the bright green of a high country pasture in June. They were wrapped up in a nice package too. She was a petite thing with delicate features, a sweet, full mouth, and hair the color of strawberry jam in the morning sun. It was too easy to wonder what it might be like to release all those silky locks and get a taste of her soft, pink lips.

Thad swiped a hand over his stubbly cheeks and brought his head down from the clouds. Yes, sir, he believed he could see some courting coming up in the very near future. The thought brought out an uncharacteristic humming of *Buffalo Gals*.

He cut the music short, though, when Grace crossed the street, passed the bakery, and instead entered Mr. Brittle's clothing store. A *men's* clothing store. That could only mean one thing, and Thad sighed, trying to expel his disappointment.

Well, it stood to reason. A pretty gal like that couldn't be unhitched. He wondered who the lucky devil was.

Lost in thought, he rubbed his thumb back and forth on the reins in his hand. Maybe everybody was right. Maybe it was time to step up, or out, and find a wife. Since nobody in Misery was pulling his trigger, he supposed he should take his brothers' advice and start visiting Sheridan more often, maybe even Cheyenne. Nick and Adam had been bugging him forever to attend the galas at the Stock Growers' Association. Thad just wasn't much for crowds, but he wasn't much keen on the idea of turning twenty-seven and gettin' beat to the altar by his brothers, older *or* younger.

That possibility hadn't concerned him much, until this moment. Losing out on Miss Grace Hendrick had changed this horse race. Snoozing at the gate wasn't going to cut it. Otherwise, he might miss out again.

And he sure hated that he'd missed out on her.

Busy with such silly thoughts, it took a minute for his brother's voice to register. "Thad," Adam hollered from the street. "Thad! Hey, quit your day dreaming."

Thad swiveled his head and saw his younger brother trotting toward him. He shrugged a shoulder in embarrassment and waved back. "Yeah, kind of got lost there for a second."

Adam, gangly and sporting shaggy golden hair, was the spittin' image of Thad when he was fifteen. His little brother shook his head in mock disgust as he brought his horse up to the wagon. "Must be that new gal in town got your head all twisted around."

"You've seen her?" Thad hadn't meant to sound so interested.

Adam chuckled. "From every angle, and the view was quite pleasant."

Thad wanted to agree, but he also wanted to change the subject. He was vaguely uncomfortable listening to his teenage brother talk about Grace like that. "You speak to the sheriff?"

Disgust clouded Adam's face as he turned an antsy horse in circles. "He's too danged old to do this town any good anymore. When's he gonna retire? He doesn't have the first clue where Bill's cattle went. He hasn't even been out looking. At least he did say the Stock Growers Association is sending another inspector."

"Brave man, considering the last one got shot." Thad glanced down the street at the sheriff's office. Phillips did seem a might long in the tooth for his job. Last time he and his brothers had joined a posse with the sheriff, the old man had spent two days *solid* complaining of his gout. Not to mention, he didn't want rustlers shooting at him. "Maybe this inspector will last longer and shed some light on the rustling." Thad's gaze roved back to Brittle's store. A young boy emerged, a paper bag tucked under his arm. He crossed the street and headed back toward them. Thad didn't recognize him. *Another stranger in town?* With all the reported cattle rustling, maybe he should pay attention. On second thought, though, this kid was so skinny that Thad doubted he could rustle up a scrambled egg. "All right, let's get on home. We'll probably catch up with Trampas. He didn't get the new horses for the remuda straight off like I told him. I found him in the Number Nine."

Adam snorted. "Is he worthless, or what?"

"Yeah, well, we'll just have to keep a closer eye on him." Thad was convinced Trampas was fudging the numbers of the herd—specifically, inflating them to hide his skimming. He'd argued with Pa about firing the bum, but the lack of proof bought the foreman one more chance...again. "Eventually, he's going to mess up, and we'll be there to catch him."

Thad snapped the reins again and steered the horses out onto the street. He pointed the team toward the Walker ranch and settled in for the twelve-mile ride home.

Grace clutched the stuffed paper bag under her arm, slipped quietly from Brittle's Men's Clothing Emporium, and hurried back toward the feed store. She widened her stride as she marched, attempting to affect a manly gate. *God, I promise, if you'll help me get this job, I'll tell this Raney woman the truth as soon as poss—*

The prayer stopped her in her tracks. She'd given up on God long ago, about the hundredth time Bull hit her. Her cup running over with hate, she figured that didn't leave any room for God. Surviving this situation and getting back to Hardy was up to her. God could go jump off a celestial cliff.

So, maybe this wasn't the best or wisest plan, but she was so hungry, and Hardy was waiting on her. To attack either problem, she had to get a job. Everything hinged on that. Desperation over the gravity of her situation clawed at her brain. The feeling frightened her. She cast a quick, sideways glance at the little saloon in town—The Number Nine—and winced.

No, no, no! Mrs. Lawson, you're going to hire me.

❦

Grace approached the man at the feed store as he stacked fifty-pound bags of oats on the loading dock. "Excuse me," she said, lowering her voice to sound more masculine. "You seen a Mrs. Raney Lawson yet today?"

The man raised up, twisted his mustache quizzically for a moment as he appraised Grace, then nodded. "She just came in to pick up her supplies. Said she'd be back in about fifteen minutes."

"Well, I reckon I'll wait." Grace hitched up her pants, thinking it a manly gesture, and ambled over to the bench. Brows still expressing his consternation, the feed store fellow rubbed his neck then went back to setting items on the loading dock.

A few minutes later, after he'd set out everything from bags of oats to rolls of barbed wire, he walked over to Grace. "You ain't waiting to see Raney about a job by any chance, are you?"

Grace nodded.

"Well, you sure are a little fella, but seein' as how Raney ain't exactly been overrun with applicants, may be you'll have half a chance."

Grace sucked in a breath. Might she really? Her heart raced at the thought.

"Least ways"—the gentleman nodded toward the street—"you'll know soon enough. Here she comes."

Grace twisted on the bench to see behind her. An older woman with a ramrod-straight posture drove a wagon toward them. A cigarette drooped from her lips as she tossed a wave to the man behind Grace. She was tanned, weathered, lean like an old chicken, and probably as tough as one. Her brown hair, streaked with gray and pulled back into a no-nonsense bun, and the deep lines in her face said the woman had seen a lot of hard times. Grace thought she saw something kind and patient in those lines as well.

Taking a deep breath, she rose to meet Raney's wagon.

"Raney, this here boy wants to talk to you about a job."

Grace cut her eyes to the man, annoyed with him for jumping in like that. She didn't appreciate his use of the word *boy* either, but she didn't give him a second chance to speak for her. "Yes, ma'am, Mrs. Lawson. I see you're looking for a ranch hand."

Raney pulled the wagon to a stop, plucked the cigarette from her mouth, and regarded Grace with a dubious expression. "You can't be much over sixteen and probably weigh about as much as a wet hen."

Grace had bought a simple flannel shirt, a pair of dungarees, brown leather boots, and a canvas jacket, all slightly oversized to hide her curves. She'd torn a strip from her petticoat to bind her breasts. Finally, she'd cut her hair with a pair of dull scissors. Yes, she probably was the picture of a scraggy, young, unkempt hooligan not worthy of a job.

Raney took another puff, put one foot up on the kickboard, and rested an elbow on her knee, as if the position helped her think. "You got any ranching experience?"

"Yes, ma'am, but I was raised on a farm."

"That mean you can ride or just feed ducks?"

Grace stepped forward, her enthusiasm getting the better of her. "I can ride as good as any man." She stumbled over that but then hurried on. "I'm strong for my size, tough, and I'll work sunup to sundown without a break."

Raney chuckled. "I'm not running a prison camp." She tilted her head, a skeptic V in her brow. "Whatta you think, Sam?"

The fellow from the feed store twisted his mustache and grinned. "Unless he's running from the law, I think you better snap him up. Maybe you get him out to that ranch of yours, he won't hear any talk of the gold strike."

Raney frowned at the joke and then wrinkled her face up at Grace. "You're not, are you?"

Grace blinked. "Pardon? Not what?"

"Running from the law?"

"Oh, no, ma'am," she answered with an almost too-exuberant shake of her head. "Never." *Just my thug of a husband.*

Raney took another drag from her cigarette. Her silence stretched out to the point Grace wanted to beg the woman to speak. Finally, she did. "I'm small. My ranch barely feeds me. But I can't run it alone. I pay $15 a month, room and board. You don't by any chance have your own horse?" Grace shook her head. "Yep, I figured as much. All right then," Raney heaved a great sigh. "Reckon I'll try you out for a few weeks."

Grace had to control herself. A girlish squeal had come within a hair of slipping out of her. Remembering who she was, or, rather, who she was pretending to be, she hooked her thumb through her belt loop. "Thank you, ma'am. You'll be glad you hired me."

"Well, I reckon that's one possibility." Raney puffed once more then tossed the little stub into the street. "What's your name, anyway?"

"Gra—" She bit that off and tried again. "Greg. My name is Greg Hen...derson."

"Well, Mr. Henderson," Raney said, locking the brake, "let's get this wagon loaded."

Chapter Four

❧

Grace didn't say much on the ride back to the Diamond R. She was afraid she might make a slip. Raney, however, didn't seem to notice. Quite a conversationalist, she kept up a steady stream of chatter as the wagon crossed treeless, rolling plains and headed toward the mountains. As the air cooled and the scent of pines wafted down to meet them, Grace learned that Raney had been a widow for three years now, only kept about a hundred head of cattle, owned fifteen hundred acres of lush, fertile land along the Crazy Woman, which was apparently a river, and all the fool men in the valley had run off to some place called Chena River to look for gold. Raney stole a suspicious sideways glance at Grace with that news, as if Chena River should mean something to her.

It didn't.

"So, what about you?" Raney asked. "You're awful young to be out here alone. Where're your folks?"

The chilly November breeze prompted Grace to

pull her jacket tighter in an effort to buy a moment. "I lost my parents in a flood in Pennsylvania."

"Aw, that's too bad. Were you young?"

"Eight. I went to live with my grandparents in Reading until—" Grace paused. *Until, at eighteen, they sent me off to school to become a teacher—my lifelong dream.* She couldn't tell Raney her grandparents had mortgaged the farm to pay for her schooling. Because then she'd have to tell her how a handsome, high-rolling Irish gang leader had flattered her senseless with diamonds, furs, and champagne. What she *could* tell her was a lie that stuck in Grace's craw. "I lived with my grandparents until I left to find work. Always wanted to see the West."

"Sounds like you're an only child?"

"Uhumm," Grace mumbled. But something made her re-think that. "No, I mean, I have a sister." The lies were piling up on each other and Grace felt ill. Why had she said that? She *was* an only child.

"Where's she at?"

Closer than you think. "We parted company in Misery. She couldn't find work here." Even when she told the truth, she was telling a lie.

"Well, it's pretty adventurous of you to come out here on your own. That takes sand." Raney's gaze drifted off to the distant mountains. "Those are the people that make it out here. Folks with sand."

Suddenly, Grace was curious about her new employer, about the things she wasn't telling her. "Ma'am, fifteen hundred acres is a lot of room for a hundred head of cattle. I don't mean to pry..."

Raney chuckled. "The Diamond R used to run

three thousand head, and we had sixteen thousand acres. When my husband died, the men wouldn't work for a woman." She paused as if recalling the details, then shrugged as if they didn't matter. "No men, no ranch. Started selling it off. I've had some drifters over the years help out, but nobody permanent. It's a size now I can manage on my own if I have to."

"Do you mind me asking what happened to your husband?"

"Jake was out checking fence one day and somebody shot him."

Grace gasped. "I'm sorry."

Raney swallowed and tightened her lips. "Almost three years now."

"When you say somebody...?"

"Never found out who or why."

Grace couldn't imagine what it must be like to live with that kind of mystery. She thought it would drive her crazy. She wanted to ask what Raney had done about it. Had she pushed the sheriff to investigate? Had she hired a private investigator? But the set of the older woman's jaw suggested it wasn't something she wished to discuss further.

Raney snatched up on the reins, jerking the wagon to a stop. She pointed to a distant hill. "That's Bill Lewis's place." A dark pillar of smoke drifted in the air. As they watched, it burned blacker and billowed faster. Raney slapped the reins across the horses' rumps and yelled, "Come on, git up!" Skillfully, she turned the wagon in the middle of the road, pointed them all back the way they had just come, and then whipped the reins again with a thunderous crack.

"Yahhh!" she bellowed and the team took off like they'd been shot out of a cannon. Grace grabbed hold of the seat and gaped in horror at Raney.

"Yahhh!" the woman yelled again, putting the horses into a thunderous gallop. A gust of wind nearly snatched the hat off Grace's head. Heart in her throat, she shoved it back down and held it in place as if she was capping a barrel of snakes.

Grace saw a road coming up on the right and braced herself, somehow sure that was the track Raney was going to take. The woman whipped the horses hard and steered them down the dusty little road at full speed. The wagon tipped, slid sideways, and then whipped back around behind the team. Grace held her breath and clung desperately to the seat, wondering if she'd come all this way just to die in a wagon accident.

Wide open and hell-bent-for-leather, Raney pushed the team to an astounding speed. The horses stretched and pounded, their hooves moving so fast they were a blur. Grace had never experienced such speed, and it terrified her, but the desperation on her employer's face told her not to question.

They crested a hill and saw a cabin engulfed in flames. Six men had formed two lines from the water trough to the fire. Working at a fever pitch, the desperate brigade dipped buckets in the water, passed them on, tossed the water, and passed the buckets back, over and over. Raney ran the wagon right up to the trough, skidded the horses to a stop, and leaped from the wagon.

"You"—she pointed at Grace as she ran around the front of the horses—"get down and work this pump."

Grace jumped to the ground, grabbed the handle, and started pumping as if *she* was on fire. Raney swooped up a bucket sitting on the ground and dipped it in the water at the head of the trough. Deftly, she exchanged her bucket with a young man, who handed off his empty vessel, and then she dipped again. Another man, older, graying, his eyes wild and round, grabbed the bucket from the man in his line. They exchanged containers, and he spun on his heels toward the fire, all in a blur of motion. The frenzied ballet went on and on and on as the inferno roared and belched hellfire. The two bucket brigades dipped and threw water with a furious beauty. Grace pumped till her arms burned like the fire was in her veins, and then she pumped some more. The inferno hissed and screamed. The heat blazed.

And then the roof collapsed in a cacophony of growling flames and snapping timbers.

Shielding their faces from the heat, the makeshift firemen backed away, lowered their buckets, and stared hopelessly at a lost cause. Exhausted, Grace leaned on the pump for support. Tears threatened, but she fought them back. She sensed someone here had lost more than a house.

Raney walked over to the man who had been fighting with real fear in his eyes, a short, stocky, middle-aged man, now covered in soot and dirt. She placed her hand on his shoulder. The look that passed between them broke Grace's heart. The man shook his head and swallowed. Raney sagged.

After a long silence, one of the young men slogged back to the trough and dipped his bucket. His movements were slow, as though his arms weighed a thousand pounds. He acknowledged Grace with a somber nod, then attacked the fire once more. Raney and the others joined in as well, but with the same weary speed.

Grace pumped the handle twice more and, as water flowed, stepped over and took a bucket, dipped it, and had it ready for the hand-off. The group worked with no sense of urgency. Grace knew a funeral procession when she saw one.

❧

After nearly two hours of dousing the doorway and entrance with more water, the young man at the head of the line dropped his bucket in the trough and left it to sink. "I think I can get in there." His solemn tone betrayed his hopelessness. "I'll go take a gander."

Raney and the others stopped their brigade and waited.

He trudged up the steps and Grace flinched against the thud his boots made on the three small steps, like the sound of the Grim Reaper entering a bedroom at midnight. He skirted a flaming beam, turned sideways to navigate some hot debris, and then paused. The man next to Raney stiffened, clenched and unclenched his fists. Raney clutched his shoulders, as if she might need to stop him from collapsing.

The man in the house kneeled and disappeared behind a glowing section of the roof. Cords of grief knotted in Grace's stomach. She kept thinking how horrible it would be to die that way, with the hellish heat and choking smoke. She heard the tall, lanky cowboy beside her swallow, as if steeling himself against the discovery.

Momentarily, the man reappeared and worked his way out of the house. He walked down the steps, shaking his head. "I'm sorry, Bill," his voice broke. "She's by the stove."

Bill tried valiantly to hold his composure, but the instant tears plowed through the soot on his cheeks, he gave in to the grief. The cowboys, all in mournful unity, removed their hats. Bill put his head in his hands and wailed. Raney locked him in a hug. For a few seconds, he accepted it, then something in him snapped. He broke away with a heart-crushing sob and rushed toward the house.

The young man blocked his path, latching onto his arm with a vice-like grip. "Bill, I can't let you see her this way." Raney stepped up and tried to put Bill back in that bear hug as the two men scuffled. The younger man shook him. "No!" And then he shook him harder. "Bill, get hold of yourself. You don't want to see her like that!"

Bill stopped. Tears ran down Grace's cheeks as she watched the man accept the news. Thankfully, his eyes glazed over with shock.

The young man waited a second more to make sure Bill was calm and then addressed Grace. "Do you have a quilt...or something...in the wagon?"

Something to wrap her in?

"There's one under the seat," Raney said gently.

Grace climbed into the wagon and rifled through the storage box. A moment later, she pulled out a moth-eaten quilt, jumped down, and walked it over to the young man.

He clutched it but didn't take it from her. "I'll need help. You up to it, boy?"

Grace swallowed. "I..." She cleared her throat and lowered her voice. "I..." But the words didn't want to work their way past the lump in her throat, so she nodded.

Raney gently rotated Bill away and led him over to the barn. Grace and the young man entered the house. She followed carefully behind him, thinking it a morbid coincidence that the man leading her through these dying flames was dressed all in black. He slid past a beam and told her over his shoulder, "Don't touch anything. It's all still hot."

Again, she merely nodded and followed him to the stove, trying to ignore the blistering heat and the smell of burned meat. She didn't make a sound when she saw the charred body lying face down on the floor, but every fiber of her being wanted to weep. The teacher in her helped her quickly assess the situation in a more clinical fashion. She assumed the woman had passed out before the flames got to her, as she was lying on the floor with both hands splayed out beside her, not curled up like a frightened child attempting to get away from the smoke and flames. Grace was somewhat comforted, knowing the woman hadn't suffered too much.

One leg was bent, her clothes and hair had burned completely off, and her entire body was black and blistered. Marks and abrasions across her back revealed that the man had moved a beam off her. Viewing these pitiful remains, Grace thought he had been right to keep the woman's husband or father out. "Who was she?"

For an instant, a wrinkle creased his brow, and Grace realized she had sounded like a girl. He shrugged, though, and said softly, "Maggie, his wife." He kneeled down to one knee, raising a hand to his mouth as if pondering how in the world to go about covering her, and shook his head. "God, if the independents did this, there will be hell to pay."

Grace helped the man gently wrap Maggie in the quilt, then slowed her pace as he carried her outside. For some reason, she hung back, as if she shouldn't be there when Bill saw his wife. She nearly slapped her hands over her ears when she heard his mournful cry, the most heart-wrenching sound she had ever heard in her life. She thought of the times she had sobbed so desperately after a beating from Bull. She'd only *thought* that was pain. What Bill was suffering—that was real pain.

Muffled voices reached her ears. Realizing they were discussing how to proceed next, she quietly wandered out onto the charred remnants of the porch. Maggie lay in the back of the wagon, the barbed wire had been removed to make room for her. Bill rested one hand on his wife's remains and wept quietly beside her. A few feet away, Raney and the young man were leaning into each other, talking in hushed tones. The other cowboys stood quietly, faces downcast, hats in their hands.

Raney looked up and saw Grace. She clutched the man's shoulder then strode over to her. "I need to go with Bill into town. We need to take Maggie..." she trailed off, shaking her head as if resisting the grief. "I'm going to let Nick here take you on to the ranch. He and his brothers help out sometimes so he can show you the routine. Feed up, and then get some rest. I'll be home in the morning."

Nick gathered up two saddled horses that had been wandering around the fringes of the disaster. Moving slowly, he heaved himself onto the back of a black-and-white pinto and led a brawny sorrel over to Grace, the cowboys parting as he came through. "We can get Bill's horse back to him tomorrow."

She nodded and hoisted herself up.

With a light kick, Nick urged his horse over to the wagon. "Bill, don't worry about anything here. We'll take care of things for you." He glanced off toward one of the cowboys, the skinny one Grace had heard swallow. "Toomey, if you need anything, don't hesitate to ask."

The man responded with a small, quick nod.

Bill made no sign he'd heard any of this. Nick didn't push it. Grace came up beside him and wanted to say something comforting to the man, but words were so worthless at a time like this. Instead, she reached down and touched his shoulder. For some reason, the action released a wave of sobbing from him. Hurting for him, Grace slowly removed her hand. The anguish in Raney's face, the crease in Nick's brow, the grief in the bowed shoulders of his cowboys, it all touched Grace. If she knew nothing else about Bill, she knew he was a decent man, and at least he wouldn't go through this alone.

Grace and Nick rode in silence for the first few miles. Her heart and mind revisited Bill's grief-stricken eyes over and over. *What will he do without her?* she wondered.

With each thud of the horses' hooves, though, her own problems inched slowly back to her. She couldn't help Bill. She could, however, help herself and her son. Unbidden, the memory of Hardy laughing hysterically over the little rocking horse he got last Christmas filled her mind and squeezed her heart. As she recalled, Bull hadn't even bothered to come home on Christmas Day after a night of gambling and womanizing.

Grace had spent most of the day with Hardy, watching him enjoy all the gifts from Santa. Then he had napped, the house had fallen silent, and she'd rambled about the Victorian mansion like a ghost, cold, empty, unseen, and trapped.

She considered the mountains surrounding her, the craggy earth rising to the cloudless blue sky, the horses casting long shadows on this wide-open plain. Grace was weary and weak with hunger but actually felt more alive than she had in years. The open spaces here filled her with a sense of freedom.

However, a glance at her clothes, the only ones she had, blackened with soot and grime, reminded her of her predicament. She could do this, *had* to do this. She just needed a few months' wages, and then she could get Hardy. Maybe they'd come back here or some other place in the West, where there was so much room to breathe.

She sensed the man stealing glimpses at her and wondered what emotions were dancing across her face. She risked a glance at him and thought maybe that angular nose and strong jaw were familiar somehow. He was tall, solidly built, wore his dark hair short, and sat in the saddle as if he'd been born to it.

He caught her staring, and she feigned sudden fascination with her horse's mane.

"Raney has a bad habit of taking in strays," he said, watching her intently. "Most of 'em don't work out too well. She really needs good help. Are you up to it?"

Grace fiddled with the horse's mane. "I'll work hard and give her everything I've got." *At least for a little while...*

Nick twitched the reins back and forth as if mulling that over. "What are you, all of about fifteen?"

"Sixteen," Grace said, trying to recall the details she'd made up for this charade. She didn't feel like thinking at the moment. She was exhausted and so hungry. In fact, her head felt a little light. It seemed to be bobbing a bit too much with the horse's motion, but she wasn't sure. "Why are you dressed all in black?"

Nick touched his lapel. "I was seeing a gal over in Rawlins. Best clothes I've got, short of a tux." He frowned at her. "But I was making a point. I've shot coyotes that were bigger than you. Work hard for Raney, or I'll slow roast you like a side of beef."

Grace nodded and closed her eyes. *Beef. A lovely idea.* She could clearly see a table before her, covered in white linen, topped with a mouth-watering array of food. *I'll have the filet mignon, with a side of broccoli swimming in cheese sauce...*

"Hey!" Nick yelled.

She frowned at his rude interruption. She hadn't invited him to dinner...

Chapter Five

T had ambled out onto the porch with a cup of coffee and leaned on a post. Evening was coming on fast, throwing the Walker ranch into the shadow of Bear Tooth Mountain. He closed his eyes and listened to the lowing of cows out in a distant pasture and the whinnying of horses in the barn. Behind him, dishes clattered as Chang cleaned up the dining room.

Good sounds, the sounds of home, but he still missed the light, delightful sound of his mother's laughter.

He heard boots behind him and knew his father was standing at the screen door. "Never get tired of looking at that mountain and our valley."

Thad nodded in agreement and twisted to greet his pa coming out the door, puffs of smoke trailing behind as he enjoyed his evening pipe. Tall, broad-shouldered, barrel-chested, Earl Walker was a legend, not only to his sons but to the whole cattle industry. He'd built the

Lazy H ranch, now the biggest spread in Wyoming, with blood, sacrifice, and tears. He'd taught Thad, Nick, and Adam to always stand up for each other, never disgrace the Walker name, and always treasure the land for which he'd paid such a high price. Thad believed the lessons had stuck.

In the distance, a steer trumpeted his displeasure over something, and Pa paused, the sound apparently triggering a thought. "These small outfits have overstepped. The rustling is out of hand. I believe the SGA is gonna have to put a stop to it."

Thad shoved his hands in his pockets, knowing his father's determined statement didn't need a response. Johnson County was losing its hold on civility. Small ranchers, clashing with big ranchers for grazing land, were getting blamed for everything, from missing cattle to bad weather. For years, Pa had been one of the few voices in the Wyoming Stock Growers Association cautioning against violence. Lately, though, his tone had changed as more and more cattle barons complained of missing cattle and run-ins with arrogant homesteaders.

Plenty of folks thought the small, independent outfits were little more than two-bit rustling operations. Thad hadn't made up his mind, but for Pa to start thinking that way, Thad could only assume the elder Walker knew something he didn't. He was willing to trust his father, even if the reverse wasn't true right now.

"I'm in agreement with your brother," Pa said, settling into his rocking chair. "Sheriff Phillips is a waste of good oxygen. Misery ever turns into anything or ever has any real trouble, he'll be over his head in two seconds."

"Maybe he'll learn a thing or two from the cattle inspector."

Earl harrumphed in disgust. "You can't *learn* a spine. You're either born with one or not."

"I reckon." Thad didn't like Sheriff Phillips, but he didn't spend much time thinking about the man, either. Thad mostly thought about work, and tomorrow, he had a long list of chores.

"When are you going over to Raney's next?" his father asked.

"As a matter of fact, I'm taking a few of the men over tomorrow. Thought we'd finish getting her bunkhouse in order before the first snow. Don't reckon she really needs it, but there's no sense in letting the place fall down around her ears, either."

"Stubborn woman," his father muttered, the pipe clenched between his teeth. "She's crazy to hold on to that place if she's not going to use it. What a waste."

Thad turned away to hide a grin. He grabbed the porch rail and wished he had a buck for every time Earl Walker fumed over Raney Lawson. There had to be more to the story, but questions were only answered with vague responses and dismissals. He'd quit asking years ago. "You never know, Pa, she might decide to re-stock, get some hands that'll work for a woman, and bring the Diamond R back into production. Dub said she's got at least one hand again. Hired him today."

Pa sat up with interest. "You say she hired somebody?"

"Dub saw 'em leavin' town. Said he's some little, bony fella, just a kid. Dub said it was all the boy could do to load a fifty-pound bag of oats."

Earl eased back into his rocker. "Well, she needs some help out there. I doubt a kid's going to be good enough to help keep things up and repaired, though. She needs to sell me all of it and move into town."

Raney had, little by little, sold Pa chunks of the Diamond R. Eventually, all of it would be absorbed by the Lazy H. Earl Walker always got what he wanted.

Since '87, he'd been on a tear, working hard to expand the Lazy H, adding sizable spreads here and there. These last few years, fortune had come Pa's way, through the misfortune of others. Deaths and disasters had allowed him to add three more ranches to their holdings.

At least he'd been able to help out his neighbors by quickly taking their spreads off their hands for fair money during some dire situations. Some of the *other* cattle barons had, to Thad's way of thinking, flat-out strong-armed a few of the smaller ranchers out of the county. Pa was patient. He didn't need to resort to violence.

Thad half-sat on the porch rail and pushed away the dark thoughts, determined to enjoy the peace. But the quiet was a rarity. One of the Walker boys was missing. "I wonder what's keeping big brother."

"Probably Angie Cole."

Both men chuckled at that, but then Thad recalled green eyes and a blue lace dress and wished he was similarly detained. His pleasant musing was interrupted by distant hoof beats coming down the road.

The horse slowed and entered the main gate. She wasn't galloping, but moving at a healthy canter. A few seconds more and Venus trotted into the front yard, Nick slouching in the saddle. Almost immediately, Thad knew something was wrong. His brother's expression was grave, and the scent of smoke filled the air.

"Something happen, Nick?" Pa asked, joining Thad at the rail. "You smell like a forest fire."

Nick shook his head as he guided his horse up to the house. He was covered in soot, and dark smudges streaked across his face. "It's bad, Pa."

Thad rose from the rail. Nick was the optimist in the family, he sugar-coated everything. Such a statement could only mean someone was dead.

"I was on my way back and saw the smoke. Bill Lewis's house burned to the ground." Nick removed his hat and pressed it reverently to his chest. "Maggie's dead."

Thad gasped. Pa clutched the rail, squeezing till his knuckles went white.

"We couldn't get her. Bill nearly killed himself trying to save her, but..." Nick trailed off and shook his head.

Pa sighed deeply and retook his seat in the rocker. He set the pipe on the small table next to him and laced his fingers together. Thad wondered if he was remembering the Indian raids, wildfires, rustlers, and grizzlies that had wounded and killed his loved ones. Such was life in the shadow of the Big Horn Mountains.

"Maggie. Bill won't be able to stand it, I think," Pa

predicted solemnly as he gazed out over their valley. "He'll go crazy without her." He ran a shaky hand over his face and rubbed his left temple.

After a moment, he rose to his feet and shoved his hands in his pockets. "Some people can't stand the price of life in Wyoming." He hunched his shoulders against the chill—and maybe the memories. "The Lazy H has been built on the blood of my kin and my broken heart, and still, we pay to live here, boys. The dues never stop coming...but if we keep this ranch going, then no price has been too high."

As their father quietly slipped into the house, Nick and Thad exchanged puzzled glances.

Nick tossed the reins from one side of the saddle horn to the other and back again. "You know, sometimes I think he loves this ranch more than us."

Thad had no response for such a stupid statement. Instead, he moved past it. "What happened at Bill's?"

Nick shook his head, running a gloved hand through dark, sooty hair before replacing his hat. "I don't really know. I saw the house from Kootenai Road, flames comin' out of every crack. It'd been burnin' a while. I raced in from the main gate and saw Bill and his boys come flyin' up from the east." He paused a long time here as Thad watched the emotions of loss and helplessness play out across his face. "Bill was runnin' around outside, screaming for Maggie. I realized he was gonna go in. The house was on the verge of collapsing. I had to tackle him. The only way I got him to calm down was by telling him Maggie wasn't in there." Nick lifted his eyes to Thad. "I lied to him. I knew she was. We threw bucket after bucket on the fire for hours." Nick clamped his jaw and shook his head. "We found her by the stove."

Thad hated it. He liked Maggie. She always had something nice to say and never went to a party without that magnificent cherry pie of hers. She was truly the light of Bill's life.

Thad couldn't say why tragedies like this happened in a person's life, but more importantly, he couldn't understand how somebody survived them without believing God held even disasters in His hands.

Knowing nothing would be solved tonight, he walked over to Nick and grabbed the horse's halter. "Here, give me Venus. I'll put her up. You go inside and eat."

Moving like an old man, Nick stepped out of the saddle and dragged himself up the steps. "Funny," he said as he crossed the porch to the screen door. "Another fire..."

Thad stroked Venus's neck. "You don't reckon rustlers..."

Nick nodded wearily, his hand on the pull. "I thought of that. But they haven't been hittin' smaller outfits like Bill's, supposedly." He opened the door but stopped again. "This is the fourth spread adjacent to ours."

"What are you sayin'?"

"I've heard talk. Talk that big outfits like us are behind all the trouble in the county, includin' the rustling."

Thad's fingers drew up into fists. He wanted to knock the tar out of Nick for even dallying with such nonsense. "Where'd you hear that? Independents like

Nate Champion? You know Pa got those other spreads in square deals and paid fair money for 'em. He's not strong-armin' anybody."

"Sure," Nick sounded exhausted, "whatever you say."

Thad snatched up Venus's reins and tugged the horse to the barn. He was sick to death of the talk of rustlers. Fires happen all the time. A million things could have started this one, a spark on Maggie's dress, an ember lodged in a shingle.

"I just think it's odd the way we found Maggie, is all."

Thad stopped but didn't turn to his brother.

"She was face down, not near a window, not curled up." Nick heaved a sigh, and an instant later, Thad heard the screen door slam shut.

An accident, Thad argued as he led Venus away. *Accidents happen. They happen all the time on ranches.*

Chapter Six

"**S**on...Son...Sonny..."

Vaguely, Grace acknowledged the pressure of a hand on her shoulder. Pushing her. Shaking her.

"Rise and shine, Buttercup."

Grace blinked, yawned, and started a luxurious stretch, but muscles she didn't know she had screamed in protest, her arms especially. She flinched and moaned and settled dreamily back onto the settee.

"What's the matter, Buttercup. You sore?"

She heard a soft swat. "Leave him alone." Raney's voice. "He worked that pump yesterday like his life depended on it."

"Liked to kill him, I guess. Nick said he fell right out of the saddle last night. Had to rustle up some grub for him."

"That explains my kitchen," Raney grumbled.

Grace rubbed her eyes and peered up at her audience. While Raney had almost motherly sympathy in her expression, Thad's smirk hinted at his childish delight. Embarrassed to have been caught snoozing, Grace leaped to her feet. "I'm sorry, I guess I fell asleep." She blinked some more, trying to expel the grogginess. "The bunkhouse is a mess."

"Well, I'm here to fix that, Sleeping Beauty." He squeezed Grace's arm. She jerked away with a grimace and he laughed. "What's the matter, kid, hard work not agreeing with ya?"

Raney *tsked, tsked* his behavior and walked into the kitchen. "Thad, that boy had a rough day yesterday. Quit funnin' him."

Grace frowned, not amused by Thad's funnin' *or* his sunny disposition. "My name is Gra-eg." She'd almost slipped.

Raney's comments seem to sober Thad some, but his good humor didn't die easily. "Well, Gra-eg," he mocked, "get some breakfast in ya and meet me out at the bunkhouse." To Grace's horror, he ruffled her hair like she was some twelve-year-old boy. Her indignation must have shown. Thad laughed again, clearly amused by her.

At the stove, Raney scowled down into an unwashed skillet. "You sure you don't want something, Thad? What about your boys?"

"No, ma'am, we all ate before we left." He walked over to the door and grabbed his hat from the hook. "Hurry up and send little man out. We'll need his help tearing down all those beams, and we're burnin' daylight."

Little man? Grace was both insulted and pleased she was pulling this off. She could, however, do without

Thad Walker's arrogance and his rambling assortment of nicknames. Grace stared at the door, unsure of what to make of the swaggering cowboy. When he'd thought she was a girl, he had been quite different. Almost chivalrous. "Is he always that—?"

"Cocksure?"

Grace heard the crack of an egg.

"Yep. He's just giving you a hard time 'cause you're young. He caught it from his brother, Nick. Now it's his turn to dish it out."

Nick? "The Nick who brought me here is his brother?"

Raney nodded as she stirred the eggs. "Yep. And he's got another one, too—Adam." She wiped her hands on her apron and reached over her head for some pepper. "They all look a lot like their daddy, but Thad and Adam take more after their mama, that light coloring and all."

That explained why Nick looked familiar. "They're going to fix your bunkhouse?"

"Yep. Storm last month dropped an oak clean through it. We can't have you living out there with a gaping hole in the ceiling." With a judicious expression on her face, Raney tasted the eggs. "Every critter for a hundred miles would be trying to curl up with you." Satisfied they would do, she heaped a manly portion onto a plate, added a biscuit and some bacon, and set it on the table. "Come get your breakfast." She poured two cups of coffee and then sat opposite Grace. "Thank you for your help yesterday. I meant it when I said you worked that pump like a full-grown man. I was impressed."

Grace shrugged. "I just did what I had to do." She picked up the fork, eager to get off the subject. "How is Bill?"

Raney shook her head as if the answer needed to be wrestled out of her. "Devastated." Her eyes glimmered, and she rubbed away the moisture. "He's a strong man, though. He'll make it. I just don't know if he'll stay out here."

Silence fell between them, and Grace heard the laughter of several men outside. Butterflies cut loose in her stomach when she thought of going out there.

"You're a mess," Raney told her, crossing her bony arms.

Grace looked down at herself. Her clothes were smeared with soot, and there was soot streaked on her hands. She'd forgotten what a sight she was. "Oh, and I slept on your settee."

The older woman dismissed Grace's concern with a wave of her hand. "That's no bother, but you need to get cleaned up a bit before you go help those boys. Otherwise, you'll never hear the end of it." She waved her thumb at the kitchen door. "There's a rain barrel out back. That'll make you presentable, at least." Deep, hard-won crow's feet creased her eyes as she took a slow sip of her coffee. "The boys'll probably go for a swim in the hot springs when they're done today. You can go, too, and take a bath."

Grace nearly choked on her egg. She cleared her throat. "A swim? Yeah, maybe. You're not paying me to swim, though, ma'am."

"And I'm not paying you to stink up my kitchen,

either. I don't care where you get it, but you're gettin'
a bath today."

※

Thad thought Raney's new hand was about the
skinniest mongrel he'd ever seen. He sure worked
hard, though, to the point Thad wondered what the
kid was trying to prove. Not that it mattered, he
wasn't his problem, and Thad respected anybody who
was really willing to put his back into it. Greg wasn't as
strong as the other men, even the ones closer to his
age, but he had a lot of heart.

And it was the dangdest thing, but Thad felt like
he'd seen this kid somewhere before. He watched him
work with another cowboy, straining to lift his end of a
roof beam and pass it up to two men on the
bunkhouse's roof. Sweat poured out of him, his face
flushed red, but not a sound of complaint slipped past
his lips.

When the men broke for lunch, Raney came out
with six glasses of lemonade. Greg immediately
helped her pass out the drinks. He thought it odd at
first that the kid had jumped up to help her serve.
Usually, only boys with a bunch a sisters ever did
that.

Then it hit him...

Greg was the spitting image of *Grace Hendrick*.

Thad rested a dusty boot on an oak stump and
watched the boy a little closer. He was afraid to hope,
but just maybe the reason she had gone into the men's
clothing store was for a relation. A brother? A cousin?

He felt the wiggle of excitement in his gut and cautioned himself against it.

Greg approached with a glass of lemonade. "Can you use a drink? Raney said the sandwiches would be out in a minute."

"You have a sister, don't you?" Thad hadn't meant to sound so sure, or excited, but the assertion was out there, so he followed through. "She's the pretty gal I met in town yesterday."

He knew his own eyes were filled with hope. Greg, on the other hand, looked like he'd swallowed a frog. "Yes, I have a sister."

"So, did she stay in town?"

Greg glanced at the glass still in his hand, and Thad took it.

"No...she left." The kid's whole face tightened and he spun the empty tray in his hands. Recognizing there was some kind of uncomfortable situation here, Thad nodded with a casual air, willing to let it drop for the time being. Greg added one last tidbit, though. "She's, uh, trying to find a job...there wasn't anything suitable for a girl in Misery."

"Is she in Sheridan then? There should be something there."

"Yes..." The boy dragged out the answer but then nodded as if remembering the details. "Yes, she's in Sheridan."

Thad couldn't help but think about the fall gala coming up in a few weeks. "A bunch of us go over for the SGA's dance next month. You'd be welcome to come along. Give you a chance to see your sister." *And me, too.*

Greg cleared his throat. "Maybe."

Thad leaned forward, resting his arms on his knee. "Listen, does your sister have a beau? I've gotta say, she really struck me."

Greg gawked at Thad. "She did?"

Thad flinched and clutched his shirt right over his heart. "I mean with both barrels. It's gonna break my heart if you tell me she has a beau somewhere."

Greg bit his lip, pondering. "What she has...is a husband."

Thad felt like a mule kicked him right in the bread basket. He lowered his face, using his hat to hide his disappointment. Knowing he should let this go, he still found questions...which led to hope. He rubbed his chin thoughtfully. "If she has a husband, what's she doing out here without him?"

Greg's brow dove hard, disapproving of Thad's questions. "You're awful nosy."

An evasive answer spurred more hope. "If she's not hitched, I'm gonna marry her."

Greg's face flushed, and his eyes bugged, but almost instantly, his surprise was replaced with a mean look. "That's my sister you're *funnin'* with. She's had enough of a hard time without some cocky, insincere cow*boy* pestering her."

Thad dropped his foot and straightened up, towering over the kid. "I appreciate you trying to protect your sister." And it was admirable. This young fellow would clearly tangle with a mountain lion if the critter disrespected his sister, but he had the wrong idea about Thad. "Now, because you haven't had a chance to get to know me, I'll let that insult slide. I am not a man who dallies with women. I really would like to see your sister again, and I have only honorable intentions."

Greg stood stock-still, as if trying to read Thad's face, or his heart. After a second, he screwed his mouth up into a murderous scowl and grunted. "I said she's married." Then the boy spun and marched into Raney's house.

Thad stumbled back and dropped onto the log stump. He felt the hope trying to die, but, at the same time, something nagged at him to keep the ember glowing. Obviously, this husband wasn't a prince among men. What was it Greg had said? *She's had enough of a hard time?*

What would make a woman and her brother hightail it out of Chicago and run all the way to Middle-of-Nowhere, Wyoming?

Something bad...

Chapter Seven

❧

Once the debris was cleared and the roof beam repaired, Grace got a good view of her new *home*. The bunkhouse was a low, rectangular log building with a tin roof. Three small windows allowed in a dismal amount of light, but it was enough. Four bunk beds, mattresses rolled up on them, lined the walls. Two bunks, splintered by the blow from the oak, had been removed to a burn pile. Grass, leaves, and pieces of the splintered roof beams littered the floor.

A simple kitchen comprised of a stove, dry sink, and cutting block took up one end of the building. For bath time, a curtain hung on a wire that could be pulled across one corner, concealing a large, round metal tub. A large, black, pot-bellied stove squatted in the shadowy center like a brooding bear. Grace couldn't imagine any quarters more different than her airy, luxuriously appointed home back in Chicago.

Regardless, the building was too much for one

person, but she couldn't complain. At least out here, she could have a lot of privacy. It just felt so...lonely.

"You sure you want to sleep out here?" Raney asked, coming up beside Grace. She studied the building's interior with a skeptical dip in her brow. "It'll be kinda..."

"Lonely," Grace dead-panned, "but I'll be all right. I wouldn't want to inconvenience you."

"Oh." Raney waved that off. "I got an extra room in the house. You might oughta sleep in there for a few nights anyhow. We've got a lot of cleaning to do in here." She flicked her dust rag at a spider web embedded in the corner of a window.

Cringing, Grace watched as the owner of the web ducked back into the shadows. Above them, a cowboy dropped in a new piece of tin over the hole in the roof, cutting off even more light. "Well, if it wouldn't be any trouble."

"No trouble at all. I've already got the room dusted and fresh sheets on the bed."

Thad appeared in the hole in the wall and ran his hands over the logs that had been trimmed off. His boys had sawed a ragged opening into a more symmetrical square. He leaned into the gloomy building and saw Greg and Raney surveying the mess. Perhaps reading their faces, he cocked his head to one side. "Raney, it's just my opinion, but if you can tolerate Buttercup there, it would make more sense to house him with you. You'll burn through less wood if you're not heating your place and the bunkhouse."

Raney worked her jaw back and forth, hiding a

grin. "Yeah, we were just talking about that." She narrowed her gaze at Grace. "You snore?"

"Not that I'm aware."

"Well, maybe. We'll see." Raney poked Thad in the shoulder as he leaned on the wall. "I still want the bunkhouse fixed good as new. Never know when I might have cause to fill the beds again."

"Or if you sell this place, it needs to be in good shape." He winked at the woman.

She jabbed him again, this time harder. "Your pa been talkin' about making me another offer?" She laughed as if the idea was uproariously amusing. "Well, I've always loved his persistence, but the Diamond R is staying with me."

"If you say so." Thad turned and grabbed the end of a four-foot-long log as one of his cowboys rolled it off his shoulder. "Greg," Thad ordered, "grab that hammer and bucket of nails right there." He and the man dropped the log into the hole, stacking it on the log beneath it. As they tapped and shoved the wood into place, Grace swept the tools up off the floor and stepped over to Thad, expecting him to take them off her hands. Instead, he pointed at the new log. "All right, this is a good, snug fit. Toenail it, and Jay and I'll go cut the rest of the logs."

Grace pondered the tools. A hammer in one hand, the bucket of nails in the other, she had no idea what to do with either. Thad frowned for a second and then tagged Jay in the shoulder. "You go get started. I'll give Buttercup, here, a carpentry lesson."

Buttercup. So help me—

Jay, a tall, gangly fella with a pronounced Adam's

apple, chuckled and touched the brim of his hat. "Sure thing, boss."

"All right...here, like this." Thad took a nail from the bucket and the hammer from Grace's hand and pounded the long iron spike in at an angle. He did one more from the opposite direction, then ruffled her hair, clearly enjoying her discomfort. "You're a smart boy. I bet you'll pick this right up. Here, try."

Raney slapped Grace on the back. "I'm going to get some cleaning rags and a broom. Good luck with that."

Grace waited for Thad and Raney to leave and then pondered the bucket of nails. Muffled voices from the roof and loud hammering convinced her that the hands up there were too busy to notice her. Rolling her shoulders, she placed a nail at an angle and tapped it with the hammer.

As she brought the hammer down for a third tap, harder this time, an explosion reverberated behind her. Squealing, she spun, tripped, and flipped over the wall, tumbling outside the building. A round-faced, pudgy cowboy peered down at her, a smoking revolver in his hand.

He slid his gun into his holster. "Weather's turnin', son. They're coming inside. You might want to make sure there ain't no more around if you're gonna sleep out here." With that, he dragged another piece of tin into place, and the whacking of hammers picked up again.

Grace scrambled to her feet and peeked over the wall. A large rattlesnake, now in two bloody pieces, twitched on the floor not three feet from where she'd been standing. Her body flashed cold, as if she'd just stepped out into the mean Chicago wind.

"What's the shooting for?" Thad asked, returning with a log over his shoulder. Feeling sick, Grace pointed. Thad leaned in for a gander and whistled in awe. "Yep, he's a fat one."

Finishing the task of toenailing was torture. Grace's hands shook, her fingers felt all fumbly, and when she hit her thumb for the fourth time, she wanted to throw the hammer across the bunkhouse. A glance at the snake kept her in check. This hole was getting fixed, in case she did have to sleep out here eventually.

The finished job wasn't going to be pretty. Most of her nails were bent. A few times, the angle was wrong, and she missed the wood completely, requiring a second nail right beside the first. She plugged away, though, not seeing much of a choice. With each log delivery, and without comment or disparaging looks, Thad went behind Grace and deftly hammered the nails, straight and crooked alike, all the way into the wood. Then he'd hand her back the tool and move on, reminding Grace of a teacher checking on a student's work. Bull would have hit her with the hammer for such clumsy mistakes.

By late afternoon, the wall was patched, the roof was repaired, and the cowboys were packing up their tools. Raney had swept, wiped, dusted, and sweated over the interior, bringing it around to something that was almost inviting.

Almost.

Grace wandered outside and tossed her hammer into a carpentry box. Stuffing her sore thumb into her mouth, she took a moment to survey Raney's ranch. The woman lived in a simple white farmhouse with a lovely, inviting porch on two sides. A tall cedar with a bench built around it shaded her front yard. A little red chicken coop and a huge barn, also painted red, sat a stone's throw from the house. A corral and round pen sat between them and the bunkhouse.

As cowboys tossed their toolboxes into the back of a wagon and retrieved their horses from the corral, Thad walked up and laid a hand on Grace's shoulder. Too used to Bull grabbing and hitting, she jerked out of his grip and spun on him, ready to block a hail of blows.

"Whoa, sorry!" Thad raised his hands in peace. Grace swallowed the fear she knew had blossomed on her face.

"I'm sorry. I don't like being grabbed."

"I gathered." Perhaps to get past the awkward moment, he changed the subject, motioning toward the bunkhouse. "Not bad toenailing, Buttercup, and what you lack in skill, you sure make up for in tenacity."

Arms as heavy as lead, joints aching, Grace was still energetic enough to demand some respect. She was as tired as any man here. "Do you have to keep calling me that? My name is Greg." Her voice rose on the last syllable. She'd nearly said the wrong name again.

He laughed and shoved her hat down over her eyes as he walked away. "Sure, Greg," he mocked again, as if the joke was never going to get old. "We're going for a swim in a hot spring on the way back to the ranch. Come with us. It ain't far."

Panic made Grace's heart trip over itself. "No, I can't!" She'd sounded a little too alarmed and kicked herself.

Thad half-turned to her, one hand resting on his gun. "Can't swim, huh?" He shoved his white hat further back on his head, giving him a relaxed, friendly air. "I can teach ya. It's a skill you should have, in case you have to cross swollen—"

"My parents drowned. I hate the water." For once, not a lie, exactly. Grace had gone swimming some over the years, especially before she left her grandparents' farm, but there was always uneasiness in her spirit. A swim sounded so inviting, filthy as she was, but there was simply no way that could happen now.

Thad drummed his fingers on his thigh and nodded. "Sorry for your loss." He stood uncertainly for a moment, as if he wanted to say more, but finished with, "If you decide to go, the pools are only three or four feet deep. Anyway, I'll see ya tomorrow."

"You will? Why?"

He tossed a wave toward Raney's house. "Raney wants us to move her herd tomorrow." He rested his hand on his hip and squinted at her. "You can ride, can't you? Ever moved any cattle?"

"Yes and no."

He frowned. "Yes, you can ride, and no, you've never moved cattle?"

Grace nodded.

"Well, then, tomorrow, Buttercup, you get your first lesson in cowboyin'."

She searched for a clever retort, but approaching hoof beats drew the group's attention to a rider trotting into Raney's yard. All the commotion and cowboy chatter halted abruptly, and Thad's expression darkened. With slow, stiff movements, as if he was barely controlling his temper, he stepped away from his men to greet the visitor.

A handsome man in his early-to-mid thirties with haunting hazel eyes reined in his appaloosa and nodded. "Thad."

"Nate."

Everyone in the yard watched the two men intently. The stranger's attention darted warily over the audience. Grace was struck by the tension brimming among these men, but especially between Nate and Thad.

"Raney around?"

"I'm right here, Nate," Raney called, drying her hands on a towel as she crossed the front porch. "What brings you over?"

Nate grudgingly pulled his gaze away from Thad and addressed the woman. "The independents are having a meeting over on the KC Thursday night, if you're of a mind to come. We're gonna talk about Bill and Maggie."

Thad took a step. "What for? You or some of the other independents thinking about buying their spread? Pa's already got plans—"

"Got plans to buy it, too?" Nate speared Thad with an accusing glare. "Bill's cattle were rustled twice before this fire. You know as well as I do that one of his men was bushwhacked. Now we're supposed to believe Maggie's death is an accident? And how convenient, the Lazy H is just gonna ride in and buy up another spread."

Thad's hands balled into fists. "If you're sayin' my pa had anything to do with those crimes, you'd better step down off that horse."

"Stop it, boys," Raney commanded. "There's been enough bloodshed in Johnson County. There won't be any on my spread. Nate, I'll see ya there."

He and Thad held one another's gaze. Grace had seen that expression over and over on Bull's face, and on those of his men—a willingness to follow anger to its worst conclusion. Given the right time and circumstances, these two could kill each other.

Apparently calling it a draw, Nate tipped his hat at Raney and rode out. The man would have to be dead not to feel the cold stares of the cowboys drilling into his back. Once he passed through the Diamond R's gate, Raney walked over to Thad. "Your pa might be innocent of some of what's going on in this county, Thad, but he ain't oblivious to it. The independents only want to be treated fair, and Nate's got good intentions. You need to believe that."

"Hard to believe that of an independent."

Raney's face formed into a disapproving frown. "You're as hard-headed as your pa."

Chapter Eight

❧

Grace stared at the skinny bed tucked away in a small room beneath Raney's stairs. The mattress, undoubtedly hard and lumpy, beckoned to her like a siren. She needed to strip out of her clothes and wash them, but the bed teased her. She gave in and stretched out on it, careful to keep her boots hung over the edge.

Her bed back in Chicago was far softer, more luxurious, and substantially larger...and it had never felt this good.

"Greg?" Raney called through the door.

Grace scrambled to her feet. "Yes, ma'am?" She took a step over and opened the door.

Raney shoved a stack of clothes at her. "Here, take these, and give me those filthy, smelly things." Hesitantly, Grace reached for the clothing, and Raney handed them off with a pat. "I'll keep rooting around till I find something that's a better fit. These were my husband's, and likely they'll swallow you, but roll 'em up, make do."

Grace flipped through the stack containing a dark blue pair of dungarees, a red, plaid button-up shirt, and a pair of white long johns. "Are you sure?"

"Unless you've got another set of clothes in that brown paper bag?" Raney eyed the bag sitting on the table beside the bed.

"Uh, no, ma'am. That's actually, well, it's kind of funny." Grace realized she sounded like a blithering idiot, but if Raney ever took a peek in there... "I accidentally got my sister's bag. There's only a dress in there." And a head-full of hair.

Raney's eyes rounded in bewilderment. "You and your sister are a pair. It's a wonder you made it out here on the same train. Well, we'll get it to her as soon as we can. You go clean up out back and leave your dirty clothes hanging on the rail. I'll wash 'em and hang 'em up after dinner."

❦

Grace stared at the tub on the back porch filled with steaming water. She wanted to shout hallelujah, but was too tired. The container was barely more than a large trough, but the warm water, oatmeal soap, and bracing November air gave her a glimpse at paradise. She couldn't recall ever appreciating a warm bath so much.

She scrubbed and soaked and drank in the view of craggy mountains in the distance. Turning orange in the setting sun, they stirred something in her soul. A leaf skittered across the porch, bringing her back to the moment. Maybe, once she had Hardy, they would come back to Wyoming.

She dried her short, unfamiliar hair and dressed quickly, the cold starting her teeth to chattering. Raney's husband's clothes were too big, but they hid any hint of Grace's curves and were blissfully warm.

She used the comb, also on loan from Raney, and ran it through her hair. A task that used to take an hour now took mere seconds. Studying herself in a shiny piece of metal that pretended to be a mirror, her skinny face and flat hair appalled her. She touched the side of her head, pulling at short sprigs, and lamented the loss of her thick, beautiful locks. But she'd survived her first day as a man. Or a boy, anyway. Thad seemed intent on reminding her she wasn't old enough to shave yet.

Thoughts of the cowboy froze her hand. He wanted to marry Grace. His intentions were honorable. Was he crazy? He was certainly handsome in a clean-faced, wide-eyed way—

"No," she whispered, dragging herself away from the mirror. She couldn't for one second contemplate anything like that. She was here, living this lie, deceiving kind people like Raney, because she *had* to get the money to get back to Hardy.

She'd do almost anything to make that happen.

His little face—chubby cheeks, dark hair hanging in his eyes—rose up in her mind. The stab of anguish hit her square in the heart.

Truth was, to get Hardy back, she'd do that one final thing, if all else failed.

But, for the time being, she'd bested Bull.

She was tired, dressed like a hobo, and passing for a scrawny boy. But she wasn't a prostitute. And she would make her way back to Hardy soon, come hell or high water. If she was lucky, Bull would never see her coming.

And Thad Walker would be a memory.

She rolled up the pants legs, rolled up the shirt sleeves, and stuffed the tail in her pants. She shuffled inside to the kitchen, and Raney had to stifle a laugh as she got a gander at her new hand. Shaking her head, she lifted a steak from the frying pan. "I won't let you make a habit out of wearing those." She dropped the meat onto a tin plate. "Thad's boys get a gander at you in 'em, I reckon you'll never live it down."

Grace clutched the throat of the huge shirt. "Yeah, I'd hate to give Thad an excuse to come up with another clever nickname. I'm so fond of Buttercup."

Raney snorted. "Don't worry about it now. Come and get your supper."

Grace ate like a starving man. The sandwiches from lunch had long since disappeared, and this steak was about the best thing she'd eaten since a petite sirloin from Delmonico's had filled her plate. She could savor the salty, juicy flavor till she died.

Raney lit a cigarette and sat back, her own meal untouched. "How are you supposed to find out where your sister winds up?"

Grace swallowed a mouthful of steak. "She said she'd write."

"Oh." Raney took a puff and then blew smoke rings for a moment. "But she doesn't know where you are."

Sweat broke out on Grace's upper lip. Why was Raney so curious? "Well, we figured, Misery being so small, it wouldn't be hard to get a letter to me."

"That's true. Thad says your sister is married. Is that true?"

An awkward silence stretched between them, and Grace figured Raney was working toward something. "Is there something in particular you want to know, Miss Raney?"

The woman exhaled smoke one last time, then leaned forward and snuffed out her cigarette in her coffee cup. "Thad says you—or, at least, that is, your sister—is running from her husband. That true?"

For a crazy moment, Grace thought about telling Raney the truth—all of it. Though her warm, brown eyes said she was curious, maybe even suspicious, they weren't without compassion. And this was the woman known for taking in strays. But what if she wanted to avoid trouble? Would she fire Grace?

"Grace is married to a professional criminal. He's... mean, I guess you'd say."

"Why is she running from him? Why didn't the two of you go back to your grandparents' farm?"

Grace's throat tightened. Her appetite disappeared, just like her dreams of becoming a teacher. Before she'd understood how Bull's mind worked, she'd made the mistake of threatening to do just that. The next day, someone had burned her grandparents' smokehouse to the ground and slaughtered five pigs. Bull had met Grace's questions and accusations with a dangerous silence. Grace hadn't talked to her grandparents since. They'd never even seen their great-grandson.

"You're out here because you're hiding, is that it?"

Grace wished Raney would drop this. Bull had destroyed every single ray of happiness in her life. Keeping her from Hardy was the last straw. She had a plan. She had her feet underneath her. Bull wasn't going to take anything else. "He doesn't know where I —I mean, we are. You won't get drawn into it. I promise."

Raney huffed, implying she was as worried about Bull as she was the mouse in the pantry. "He might be mean for Chicago, but he ain't seen mean till he comes to Johnson County."

Grace saw a chance to change the subject and leaped on it. "That man that was here today, Nate... why was there so much tension?"

Raney's expression changed to something sad and hopeless. The curiosity about Grace that had sparkled in her eyes faded away. "There's a war going on in this county, the likes of which I've never seen. Men killing each other for land and cattle, power and money. But there's a fight going on for independence as well."

She crossed her arms and leaned on the table. "Most of the big outfits are owned by Scottish and English conglomerates." Her voice rose with passion, and she poked the table with her index finger. "They come in here with their high-and-mighty attitudes, begrudging the independents, their small herds, and a hundred acres of land. The more land I've sold, the more they've treated me like I don't have a right to be here." She slammed the table, startling Grace. "Well, this ain't England, and Wyoming is no colony of the Crown."

"I take it this Nate is an independent then?"

"Oh, he's more than that. He's a fireball and a thorn in the side of every cattle baron in this state. Ever since they lynched Jim Averill and Ella Watson—"

"They lynched a woman?"

"Ella was a friend of mine and Nate's. A good girl, no matter what the newspapers said. Liked her whiskey and cigars, but she was a good, decent person."

All at once, Grace felt a vested interest in this cattle war. How many times had Bull put his hands around her throat, fingers threatening to squeeze the life from her? She doubted the leap from beatings to murder was very far.

Shaking her head, Raney twirled her fork around in her mashed potatoes. "Every independent is not a rustler, but the barons are painting it that way, and they own the newspapers. Ella was tried and convicted in the press and her murder excused." She snorted in disgust. "Helluva note."

Grace wondered about Thad and his animosity toward Nate. As if reading her thoughts, Raney dropped her fork and pushed her plate away.

"Earl Walker used to be a good man. I'm not so sure anymore. I think all the cattle barons have blood on their hands, and I fear Thad has a rude awakening coming about his pa."

Chapter Nine

❧

"Luckily, this is a small herd." Thad raised his arm and swished a quirt back and forth, gently urging the herd onward. His horse ambled forward at an easy pace as the cattle lowed and grunted and meandered through the short, dry grass. Beside him, Greg shifted in the saddle and scanned the rolling, open horizon.

Thad saw something in the kid's face he couldn't peg, maybe because every time he looked at him now, he saw *her* face. Regardless, the kid was sweating bullets. Thad needed to try to convince him to relax, for both their sakes. The last thing he needed was a jittery greenhorn on his hands. Even a hundred head could stampede, and he was never going to let that happen again.

Trying to reassure Greg, he motioned at the dip in the hills before them. "They know where to go, and we can usually get 'em there in a couple of hours." Another few minutes and they would smell the water.

God, please let the creek be down.

The golden sunshine and well-munched grass quivering in the November breeze reminded him of the recent rains. He sneaked another peek at the rawboned boy next to him. High water would mean a cold, miserable crossing. "We have to get over the Crazy Woman with them. You good with that?" he asked tentatively.

Greg hunched his shoulders. "Is it deep?"

"No, but it's gonna be cold. And I can see where it'd be a little scary to a city kid."

Greg opened his mouth as if to argue, but then clamped his lips shut.

"Hey, I don't mean anything by it," Thad ducked his head in apology. "I've lived out here my whole life, been in the saddle since I was two, but it's easy to make mistakes. Shoot, I lost a herd a few years ago."

Greg's brow wrinkled. "What do you mean *lost?*"

Thad rubbed his neck, wishing he hadn't mentioned the disaster, one he was still trying to get his father to forgive...and forget. "Lost control." He hated the icy nausea that accompanied the memory. "They stampeded. The herd was blind with panic, but I thought we could turn 'em." He shook his head, his soul full of regret. "They roared over the crew like an avalanche."

"Oh." Greg went back to the herd, eyeing it suspiciously, as if it might explode into a stampede any second. "They killed some of your men?"

"Three." Three funerals. Three widows. Thad resituated his hat and wished he could undo the day just as easily. Get those men back. Get his father's trust back. Maybe when he did, Pa would let Trampas go.

"That's awful. But I'm pretty fast when I have to be."

Thad appreciated the attempt to lighten his mood. "And when *I'm* done with you, you'll be a cowboy fit for any of the best outfits."

Greg muttered something under his breath that sounded to Thad like *that's what you think.* "What?"

"Um, I said, I need a drink." The kid reached for the canteen hanging on the saddle.

"I guess I'll have to teach you to throw a lasso, too, huh?"

Greg swallowed his sip. "I'm not really a city kid. I grew up on a farm, but there wasn't much of a need for lassoing pigs and turkeys." He wiped a slender hand across his mouth and studied Thad, not attempting to hide his suspicion. "Why are you so bent on helping me? Just to get to my sister?"

Thad moved his horse right with a simple tug on the reins and brought a straying cow back into the herd. "I've known Raney my whole life," he said over his shoulder. "She was best friends with my ma. She was there for us when Ma contracted a fever and passed. We were there for her when her husband was murdered." He swished the quirt a few more times at the heifer, then reined in again beside Greg. "I owe her. She's had some hard times and worthless help since Jake died. But you," he tsked, "I've got a feeling you might work out. Your sister is a bonus, I hope."

"I told ya she's married. Do you not understand the meaning of the word?"

"Women can get divorced when they're in bad situations. If the two of you are out here, it must be pretty bad."

The kid's mouth fell open, apparently in shock, but then he shifted his gaze back out over the living river of animals. "You don't know anything about...things."

"So, tell me." Greg dropped his gaze to his saddle horn. Thad reached out and firmly lifted the boy's chin. "You're on the back of a horse in the middle of a herd of cows. Do your thinkin', but never take your mind off business. I should know." Greg accepted the advice with a subtle, humble nod.

Thad withdrew his hand but, for the sweep of an instant, recalled with perfect clarity eyes as green as Oriental jade, silky, strawberry hair touched with honey, and a pretty, pert nose. The resemblance between brother and sister was downright spooky. Probably not something a young boy wanted to hear. Except for the short, scraggly hair, bony frame, and floppy hat, he was the mirror image of Grace.

He scolded himself for forgetting his own advice and went back to the job at hand.

"Is that how it happened?" Greg asked gently. "You took your mind off your business?"

Thad exhaled and searched the grassy plains in front of them. Watching the herd should be second nature, and yet, he found himself fighting a distraction. He couldn't afford that.

"I thought we were gonna talk about you." Silence met his comment, and he knew Greg was waiting. Thad fought the urge to talk, but something about this kid pulled it out of him. "My brother Nick and I had a fight. Over nothin' really. I was mad at him for coming home half-drunk. I accused him of letting me do all the work while he chased skirts." It seemed like such a stupid complaint now, certainly nothing to forfeit lives over. Thad resituated his hat again and chided himself for the nervous habit. "Anyhow, I was busy counting the ways I was going to murder Nick when the storm hit. I never even noticed till the wind changed. Then the lightning struck, and all hell broke loose."

"I don't know much about cattle, but don't stampedes happen? What were you supposed to do?"

"I sent three men out to turn the herd. We all should've gone. I don't know what I was thinking." For the millionth time, Thad second-guessed the decision. "I can't afford any mistakes like that again. Life is hard enough out here without being stupid."

The pause in the conversation lasted a spell before Greg finally asked, "Speaking of a hard life, that fella that lost his wife yesterday. Is he all right?"

Thad sighed. He heard Pa's voice reminding him about the dues Wyoming demanded. Sometimes, they were mighty steep. "My pa is gonna talk to him. I don't know what Bill's gonna do. Without Maggie, I think we'll be hard-pressed to keep him from blowing his brains out." He continued scanning the area around them like a soldier on guard-duty. No clouds. No coyotes. A content herd. "Pa might offer to buy his spread. I know he'd like to have it. I have a feeling Bill might sell it and high-tail it out of here."

"Just like that fella, Nate, said."

Thad whipped his head around. "Nate Champion is a troublemaker."

Greg seemed to weigh that then took his attention back to the herd in front of them. Angry he'd let the mention of Nate disrupt his focus, Thad did the same.

"Raney thinks highly of him. You think highly of Raney. That seems at odds."

Thad tightened his jaw, waited out his irritation before he spoke. "I love Raney, but I stand with my pa. Now, we're gonna get these cattle across the creek, then you go on back to the Diamond R. I've got to go into town."

"The woman who was lynched. Was it really a lynching?"

For some reason, Greg was intent on going down bad roads. Thad reined his horse to a stop, followed by Greg. "Yes."

Ella was a fine, likable woman with a big heart. Thad had never really been able to swallow the story of her being a rustler or a whore. Then, the way witnesses died or went missing before the trial had left an acid taste in his mouth. And the rancher who had sparred repeatedly with Ella had wound up with all of her holdings.

No arrests, no trial...admittedly, no justice.

But that was down in Natrona County. Thad couldn't do anything about injustices down there. Johnson County and the Lazy H were enough to worry about, and Lord willing, there would always be justice in this county. "Ella was an independent, and they give us big outfits a hard time, with their rustling and fences, but she didn't deserve that. Bothwell and the others, they think they got away with it, but hell is a real place, and I won't shed a tear when they depart for it."

"Then is it possible Maggie *was* murdered?"

Thad worked his jaw back and forth, tamping down his irritation with these questions. "Why are you so curious about all this?"

Greg bit his bottom lip and shrugged. "Just wondering what would motivate a man to kill a woman, I guess. Cows seem a pitiful excuse."

"Murder has been happening ever since Cain and Abel. Some men will do it at the drop of a hat. Cows are just that—an excuse. It's really about power. Anything to get it. Anything to keep it."

Tired of this subject, Thad cut his horse off to the right and forced the herd to stretch out. The creek came into view and he breathed a sigh of relief. High, but not dangerous. Not over the tops of Greg's stirrups in the worst spot.

He watched for a moment as the cows meandered into the water, then trotted back over to Greg. "Get 'em through this, and then all we have to do is settle them in those hills over there."

Greg's face had drained of any color and he nodded like his head was tied on too tight.

"You all right?"

Again, the jerky nod.

Thad drummed his fingers on his saddle horn. He needed Greg to cross *alone* and steer the herd so he could stay on this side of the river and bring up the rear.

Apparently, he was crossing twice.

"Nothin' to be nervous about. I'll cross with ya. Then go race ahead of the herd and turn 'em. You good with that?"

Once more, only a nod. Thad tamped down a sigh.

"All right."

They entered the water together, cows to one side, water and cottonwoods on the other. Greg swallowed. "It's not very deep?"

Thad almost chuckled at the hope in the boy's voice. "Nah. Maybe up to Dandy's belly. The current is pretty strong, though. If your horse stumbles, you're liable to go for a quick swim, which'll make for a long ride home."

"Got it." Greg urged his horse on and leaned forward in the saddle, eyeing the water suspiciously, a death grip on the reins. He acted like a man convinced of imminent disaster.

"Relax. This'll be an easy crossing."

The words were barely out of Thad's mouth when Dandy stepped on a rock that shifted beneath his hoof. The horse struggled for his footing, floundering and splashing as more river rocks rolled away. Suddenly, the horse sank a good foot deeper as he slid into a hole, bringing water all the way to the stirrups. The unexpected jerk and cold water threw Greg off balance. As Dandy attempted to leap from the creek, the boy flipped off the back and went under with a decidedly high-pitched holler.

Thad flinched and whistled with no sympathy. That water was cold enough to cause a heart attack. He shivered at the thought and spurred his horse. Greg leaped out of the water, gasping and sputtering.

Thad grabbed him by the collar, snatched him over his saddle, and lunged for the bank.

Hitting dry land, Thad tossed the kid to the ground. He collapsed like his legs were numb. His lips were already blue.

"Yep, you've got a long ride ahead of you." Thad undid the bedroll at the back of his saddle and tossed it to Greg. "My favorite poncho's in there. I want it back."

The glare Greg hit him with could have knocked a lesser man out of the saddle. Laughing, Thad touched the brim of his hat, kicked Bo, and headed off toward town. He felt a little guilty. But, truthfully, it was things like this that would make a tough cowboy out of an underweight, greenhorn kid.

Before Thad disappeared over a hill, he risked a glance back. Greg was up, wearing the poncho and pulling himself into the saddle.

Yeah, he was gonna be just fine.

Chapter Ten

❧

Raney *thinks highly of him. You think highly of Raney.*

For some reason, that observation dogged Thad all the way into Buffalo. Pa hadn't come right out and said anything nasty about Nate Champion, but he'd made it pretty clear the man was nothing but a malcontent and troublemaker. Between trying to start a separate stock growers association and blaming the big outfits for rustling their *own* cattle, Champion was a burr under everyone's saddle.

Thad rode up to the Occidental Hotel and dismounted. Raney had liked Ella, as well. Swore she was a good, decent, hardworking woman. She'd been livid over the murder and wrote some fiery letters to several of the papers, letters only one newspaper had run, the Buffalo Bulletin.

"Well, good afternoon, Thad. What brings you to Buffalo?"

Thad followed the voice of Doc McCain coming

out of the hotel, patting his stomach. A tall man with white hair and a white beard, he also preferred white suits. A strange choice, but somehow, the man managed to keep them nearly spotless.

"Afternoon, Doc." Thad wrapped the reins around the hitching post and stepped up on the boardwalk. "Came to check on some paperwork at the court-house. How are things?" He stuck out his hand for a shake.

Doc's grip was limp. "I'm sorry to say, Jasper and I prepared Maggie's body for burial this morning. Such a terrible tragedy. I will miss her." He reached inside his breast pocket and pulled out a cigar. "But Jasper built her a lovely casket. Lined it with blue velvet."

Thad stared at his boots and heard the match strike. Frustrated by nagging doubts, he wanted to walk on, grab a bite of lunch, and go to the court-house. Go about his normal business, but for some reason, he couldn't. "Doc, was Maggie's death an accident?"

Doc nearly dropped his cigar. He glanced around as if someone might be listening and brushed ashes off his lapel. "Why would you ask a thing like that? Fires happen all the time." The older man's gaze steadied, and a somber, warning tone entered his voice. "Besides, the dent in her skull could have been caused by her fall."

Thad's shoulders sagged. "But it wasn't."

"In this town, with all the feuding that's going on, Thad, the simple answer is her dress caught on fire and she died in the blaze. There's no way to prove anything else, and I wouldn't try. It'd be a good way to wind up dead."

Thad leaned on the counter in the tax office and filled out the check with the payment, but his hand worked on its own. His thoughts kept circling back to Maggie.

Thad had ridden into Buffalo to handle the humdrum tax filings for the ranch, but now he couldn't shake the sense he was into something over his head. Doc's warning about Maggie and what might really be going on around here nagged at him, nagged at him like a screechy, old fishwife.

Finished with the check, he slid it across the counter to Ray Calhoun, the graying, soft-spoken clerk of court. "Thank you, Ray."

"Thank you, Thad."

He nodded at the old man and ambled back out into the late afternoon sun.

Standing on the steps of the courthouse, twirling his hat, Thad told himself to get on home. There was nothing in Buffalo he needed to worry about.

But that felt like a lie.

For Maggie's sake, he could ask one simple question and know which side of things to come down on. He scratched his nose and nodded.

Fine. One question.

"Sheriff," Thad slapped his hand into the beefy paw of *Red* Angus and received a friendly smile in return. Thad hadn't expected it to be so easy to find the lawman, but here he had come sauntering down the boardwalk. No way to avoid him.

"Thad, good to see ye, laddie."

A short, stocky fella with blazing red hair and a thick mustache, the Scotsman had proven himself a brave, reliable lawman. That, despite an early start in Buffalo as a frequent patron of saloons and soiled doves.

Side by side, the two continued walking north.

"What brings ye into town?"

"Filing some tax paperwork." Thad removed his hat, ran his hands through his hair, and replaced the Stetson. "Listen, I wanted to ask you..." He trailed off, and the two men stopped.

Angus faced him and lifted a copper-colored brow. "Aye, ye've somethin' on yer mind?"

Thad blew air through his lips, acknowledging the stupidity of this question. "Off the top of your head, best guess, how many head of cattle have gone missing in Johnson County?"

The sheriff's other brow shot up. "Do ye want the count from the Cheyenne papers...or the truth?"

Thad pulled away from the man's penetrating blue eyes and scanned the street. "It was a simple question."

Sucking on his cheek, the sheriff studied Thad as if weighing whether to bother with him. After a moment, he nodded and resumed his walk. Thad didn't want to follow, but he did.

"Five livestock cases have been adjudicated this year," Angus said as if reciting a legal docket. "They involved a grand total of twenty animals—five horses, fifteen head of cattle, four different men. The plaintiffs in all five cases were big cattle operations. All five defendants were owners or employees of small, independent outfits, and all five were acquitted."

"*Five* cases?" Thad was stunned. "Then the rustlin', the *deprivations* to the herds that Wolcott and the others are always hollerin' about, they're just...?"

"Hmmm." Angus scratched his chin. "I think the word ye're searchin' for is *lies*."

"But the newspapers..."

The sheriff also had built a reputation for cutting to the bone with the truth. He didn't disappoint. "...are bought and paid for by cattle barons and politicians. They print what they're told to print."

Thad shoved his hands in his pockets and shook his head, a little disgusted with himself for having buried his head in the sand. "All just to keep out homesteaders?"

"Men build kingdoms, Thad. It's the way the good Lord designed us. Big, little—size dusna matter. It seems the bigger the kingdom, the more willing a man becomes to protect it." Angus's face clouded. "I will say, though, I've never seen such an organized... *campaign*, if ye will. The papers are being used to paint the whole of Johnson County as a den of thieves. According to them, the acquittals prove that. There is no law here, they say." He pursed his lips and drummed his fingers on his thigh. "I believe they're buying themselves cover for something with all these lies, Thad. If ye get wind of it, I would appreciate knowing."

꩜

Grace had seen enough of Thad Walker for one day, thank you, especially after the humiliating rescue from the creek, followed by two miserable hours in the saddle. If not for his poncho, she would have frozen to death while he rode off joking about how nice the weather was for a swim.

When she finally dragged herself back to the ranch, Raney told her to throw her belongings in her saddlebag. Grace would be going along for a meeting in Cheyenne. First, though, the two would be joining the Walkers for dinner, and they were taking Bill with them.

Now, the three of them sat on the wagon seat, quiet, lost in solitude as they rolled across the autumn-tinged hills. Grace barely had the circulation back in her toes. Still, she didn't have Bill's problems. He looked terrible. Beneath his hat, his skin was sallow and paper-thin. Gray smudges filled the hollows under his eyes. He still smelled of smoke. She'd never seen a more broken man.

The wagon rolled through the gate welcoming them to the Lazy H. The Walker house came into view, surprisingly, a less impressive home than Raney's. A simple, single-story structure of clapboard siding, its three brick chimneys, all belching smoke, rose above the tin roof. Milled white posts supported a long, plain front porch. The lone rocking chair near the front door moved eerily in the breeze.

A tall, barrel-chested man burst through the screen door to welcome them as Raney drove the wagon in. Thumbs tucked into his belt, he stopped at the top of the porch steps and nodded at the group. "Raney. Bill."

Raney pulled the reins back, stopping the horses. "Earl. This is my new hand, all one hundred pounds of him. Greg, this is Earl Walker."

Earl barely acknowledged Grace as he hurried to help Raney down. Bill climbed down behind her, and the Walker patriarch grasped his hand in a friendly way. "It's good to see you, Bill. I'm sorry for the circumstances." Bill responded with a soft grunt. Earl laid a hand on his back and glanced at Grace. "Boy, take the wagon over to the barn. I'm sure these horses could use some water."

Boy? Offended but trying to hide it, Grace scooted over and grabbed the reins. As her party disappeared inside, she trotted the horses over to the barn. Nearby, cowboys decorated the front porch of the bunkhouse like vines, draping themselves over rocking chairs and porch rails, smoking, chewing, and spitting. Grace heard the chuckles as she rolled by but ignored them. She probably was quite a sight. *All one hundred pounds of her.* Most of the cowboys she'd met so far had at least another seventy-five or so pounds on her, even the short ones.

She steered the horses to the trough and set the hand brake.

Now what was she supposed to do? Should she go inside? Raney had asked her to come along, but something about Earl Walker didn't exactly welcome the hired help.

"We get some pretty high winds in this part of Wyoming," a man drawled from somewhere behind her. "You don't put some meat on those bones, you're liable to wind up in Kansas."

Grace glanced over her shoulder. A tall, lanky cowboy descended the bunkhouse steps and leaned back on the hitching post. Licking a cigarette, he grinned at her. A man out for sport. The demeanor was all too familiar.

Ignoring him, she jumped down and sidled over to the horses, who were enjoying the cool water.

"Tell me," the man said, sauntering toward her. "You get full wages when you start shaving?"

Grace took a deep breath and met the man's gaze but kept her peace. Much more, though, and she was joining Raney, and Earl Walker would just have to entertain an extra guest.

The ranch hand laughed and raised his eyebrows. "My, that's a pretty intimidating look. Reckon you can back it up?"

"Hey, Trampas," one of the other cowboys called from the porch. Grace recognized the man's bobbing Adam's apple. Jay. "Thad calls him Buttercup."

Trampas hooted and slapped his leg. "Now that's funny." He leaned down into Grace's face. "What's up, Buttercup?"

Done, she patted a horse goodbye and made to march past Trampas. She wasn't surprised when he grabbed her arm and stopped her. "Whoa, there, little fella, we're just having some fun. No need to run off."

She debated her response. If she fought back, then, like Bull, this man would lay into her. She should keep her mouth shut, but a *man* who showed fear might never live it down, and then her life would only get harder. "I get it. I'm small and scrawny. Why that's so funny, I don't get." She glanced at his hand on her arm. "But if you don't take your hand off me, mister, you're going to draw back a nub."

Trampas's face darkened. His lips tightened, and so did his grip. "Boy, I can stomp you into the ground and wipe you off my shoe faster than—"

"Trampas, there a problem here?" Thad's irritated voice singed the air from the main house to the bunkhouse. Cowboys straightened up, fidgeted, and found things to stare at on the ground.

Trampas hesitated only a moment then released Grace. "No, sir, just introducing myself to Raney's new hand." He took a small step back as his boss crossed the yard to join them but kept his gaze on Grace.

The set of Thad's jaw and the curl in his fist revealed a man who wanted a fight, if the foreman cared to oblige. He nudged Trampas's shoulder, stealing his attention. "I'm disappointed in you, Trampas. What's next? Taking candy from babies?"

The ranch hand's eyes darted to the main house, then back to his employer. He licked his lips as if pondering his response. "Just havin' a little fun is all."

"Fun's over. Greg, supper's ready. Raney sent me out here to fetch you." He nudged Grace away from Trampas. As she passed by, she heard Thad whisper, "Any time, Trampas."

Then he was beside her, ushering her toward the main house.

"You did right. Trampas thinks he can run over you, he won't quit. And the men'll respect that you stood up for yourself."

Dressed in a crisp white shirt, brown tweed vest, and camel-colored trousers, Thad didn't look a thing like the dusty cowboy who had taught Grace to toenail lumber or move cattle. His blue eyes glimmered with a friendly welcome for her, but she saw concern, too. "You've got friends all over this county, don't you? Who is that fella?"

"Trampas, our foreman." Disgust laced his voice. "Pa hired him a couple of years ago. The only thing he ever did that I respected was he quit Bothwell after they killed Ella. Said he couldn't stomach lynching a woman."

"Good to know the man has standards."

Thad shoved his hands in his pockets as they climbed the steps to the main house. "Pretty low ones, in my opinion. I think he takes advantage of Pa. And I suspect he's rustling cattle, but we haven't been able to prove it." He pulled the door open for Grace. "But I will."

Chapter Eleven

❦

For a moment, Grace waited for Thad to pull out her chair at the dinner table, earning her a puzzled glance from him as he sat down. Grace cleared her throat to cover the blunder and grabbed her chair. One little slip like that and this whole lie could come apart.

Seated, she grabbed the napkin off the table and placed it in her lap, taking in the company at the table. Earl Walker, a big man with a booming voice, sat commandingly at the head. Thad took the other end of the table, Raney and Bill were to Grace's left, and the other Walker sons sat opposite her.

With the brothers side by side, Grace could see the family resemblance among them. Though Nick had dark hair, all of the Walker men had startling blue eyes, strong features, and hair in need of trimming. Broad, muscular shoulders were a family trait as well.

Everyone at the table locked hands and lowered their heads. Surprised, Grace copied them but peeked as Thad led them in a quick dinner blessing. Then he flicked his napkin open and motioned to his brothers. "Greg, that's my little brother Adam..."

Grace noted the young man's hair was as blond as Thad's, cropped the same way as Thad's, and he wore a vest similar to Thad's.

The teenager nodded politely and reached for the creamed corn. "Nice to meet ya, Greg."

The case of hero worship was advanced and she couldn't help but be amused by it. "Likewise."

"And that scoundrel is Nick, the older brother."

Nick, again dressed in black, took the bowl of corn from Adam and nodded at Grace. "Good to see you again, Greg. You recovered from that stint at the pump?"

The moment the words left his mouth, activity at the table froze. Bowls hung in mid-air. Nick flinched and dipped his head. "I'm sorry, Bill. That was a pretty dang stupid thing to say."

Bill, staring morosely at his empty plate, blinked as if coming out of his daze and reached for his glass of water. "It's all right, Nick."

"You need anything, Bill, you know we're here for you." Earl scooped green beans onto his plate as food continued to circulate. Raney held a platter of fried chicken out for Bill, and didn't move until he took a leg and set it on his own plate.

"I appreciate that, Earl."

A stubborn tilt to her chin, Raney dropped a helping of mashed potatoes and green beans onto the man's plate. He made no move to touch the food. "You need to eat something, Bill."

He obediently picked up his fork but merely held it in his hand. Earl contemplated the man for a moment, then switched his gaze to Raney. Grace didn't miss the subtle softening in his eyes or the way his voice lowered a touch as he addressed the woman.

He asked about things out at her place, and eventually, the conversation thawed in general, though everyone was cognizant of Bill's recent loss. He didn't contribute much to the conversation, just added a nod here and there. His loss tugged at Grace's heart. Did he wonder if Maggie had been murdered, or did he accept her death as an accident?

Finally, a short, rotund ranch hand brought in two apple pies and a pot of coffee. The scent of apples and cinnamon filled the room, and Grace thought of Hardy. Her chest constricted as she remembered how much he loved fresh apple pie topped with vanilla ice cream.

Thankfully, Earl's deep voice pulled her back from the memory. "Thad, how's the yield coming out so far this year?"

Thad wiped his mouth with his napkin and cleared his throat. "We've got about two hundred calves. We're down about fifty from this time last year."

"Fifty?" Earl leaned an elbow on the table and hid his mouth behind his fist. "You sure about those numbers?"

"Pretty sure."

"I rode with him the second time," Nick said, setting down his fork. "The count's good." The firmness of the statement sounded as if he were defending Thad.

Earl scratched his chin. "It's off a fair amount from Trampas's number."

The brothers swapped uneasy glances. Thad rested his hands on the table, tapped his fingers, and waited on his father with a blank face. Grace sensed the tension.

Earl leaned back and waved a biscuit at his son. "Do your count again."

The expressions on Thad's and Nick's faces didn't change exactly, but there was a hardening that happened, as if the determination to hide their true feelings outweighed everything. After a moment of awkward silence, Adam tagged Thad on the shoulder. "Get your guitar out, Thad. Liven up this party."

Before Thad could respond, Earl threw his napkin on his plate. "That guitar is tomfoolery. Why don't we retire to the drawing room for a few snorts of brandy?"

Adam dropped his gaze to his plate. He did not hide his disappointment nearly as well as his brothers. Nothing in Thad's expression gave away his thoughts, but his throat rippled, and Grace caught the slightest tightening in his jaw. Disheartened to see so many similarities between Earl Walker and Bull Hendrick, Grace rose and followed Raney to the other room.

The group settled quietly in the drawing room, one richly appointed in velvet and dead animals. The firelight glittered eerily in the eyes of stuffed antelopes, bears, and cougars. Bill, Thad, and Raney took seats near the fire while Earl poured drinks at the bar. Adam and Nick resumed a chess game. Based on the position of the pieces, Adam had his older brother on the run.

Grace tried to settle out of the hum of things and seated herself at the piano. She ran her hands over the frame but didn't touch the keys. She loved playing but didn't think that was necessarily a skill a rangy, underweight cowboy should brag about.

Earl passed out the brandies to the adults, then strode over and rested an arm on the hearth. Bill leaned back in the ornately embroidered Bergere armchair and sighed, staring deeply into the dancing flames. His anguish caused Adam's hand to pause. For a moment, the crackling logs were the only sound in the room.

Earl took a sip of his drink then dropped down on the settee next to Raney. He leaned forward and rested his elbows on his knees. "Bill, I said we want to help. What do you need? Do you want to keep running your spread? Do you want me to get you a foreman so you can go back east? Do you want to sell it outright? The longer you put off these decisions, the more things'll get squirrelly with your cattle. No sense making it easy for the rustlers."

"And your men are likely wondering, Bill." Thad shifted in his seat, leaning forward on his elbows as well. "Wondering whether they need to stick around or not."

Raney nodded. Her expression was soft, comforting, perhaps reminding Bill he was among friends. He returned the nod. "I have a good crew. I owe them. You're right." He shifted to Earl. "You're the only SGA member I would sell to. You've always been decent to me and given me a fair shake. Some of your men rode with mine both times my herd was rustled. I appreciate that you've always treated me like a neighbor, not a vassal, like some of those other outfits."

Earl shrugged, humbly lowering his head. "You've fought Indians, thieves, and disease to keep your land. Not like those Johnny-come-lately homesteaders. You and me hacked our spreads out of the wilderness."

"You know what my spread is worth. Will you pay that? And keep my men on?"

"Give or take." Earl grinned and thrust out his hand.

Bill stared at the outstretched hand as debate raged on his face. "We had a lot of hopes and dreams for that place. Then the girls got married and moved away. Wasn't anybody but Maggie and me then. Now there's only me. And I want to see my grandkids grow up." He took Earl's hand. "Guess my ranching days are over. I'm moving to Boston."

"I'm truly sorry," Earl said, squeezing Bill's hand, "about everything. You and Maggie were good neighbors. We're heading to Cheyenne tomorrow for some meetings. Why don't you go with us as far as Casper, and we'll see my lawyer?"

"Hey, did you know Susanna Kinsey is performin' at the Opera House in Cheyenne?" Adam blurted out, jerking Nick out of deep next-move contemplation. Everyone in the room frowned at the outburst, taken aback by it. The boy shrugged sheepishly and tried to explain his enthusiasm. "Well, that fella Warren just remodeled it and all. It's supposed to be a heck of a place now, and she's gonna do some play written just for her." He trailed off, his cheeks blazing.

"Yeah," Raney mused, "Cheyenne is quite the city. They're trying to rival Chicago, what with electric lights and telephone service."

For the first time that night, Grace heard something that truly piqued her interest. Telephones. They had telephones in Cheyenne, as did Bull's mansion back in Chicago.

Her brain spinning with schemes for getting down to Cheyenne, Grace excused herself from the room to visit the outhouse. Singing crickets and wailing wolves serenaded her as she thought about the possibility of a telephone call. Oh, to hear Hardy's voice again. What about the risk? How much should she say if she could get him on the phone? Maybe she wouldn't say a word. If she could simply hear him say *hello*, that could be enough for a while.

Lost in these hopeful thoughts, she glanced up... and jerked to a stop, stunned by the sight overhead. So many stars littered the night sky there was nearly more brilliance than darkness. She'd never seen such a wealth of celestial lights scattered throughout the heavens. Seemingly in chaos, the sky glittered from horizon to horizon like a diamond-encrusted tapestry. Twinkling, shining...

Moving? She gasped as a shooting star streaked across the sky.

This glorious panorama of star upon star upon star hovered over her, and she was moved by it. There was nothing chaotic or accidental in the speckling of lights. Inexplicably, she sensed the presence of Love out there, like a Master Painter creating his finest work of art for the sheer pleasure of his beloved.

As she gazed up in awe, the heavens revealed more magic. A shimmering light grew in the north, glimmering first green, then orange, then blue, weaving its way southward across the sky. Her mouth fell open. This light shimmered magically overhead, undulating with the change of color.

What the—?

"The northern lights."

She squeaked and whirled, startled by Thad's deep voice. Her hand clutched at her chest as if to keep her heart in place. Aware she was acting like a silly girl, she finished off the near-scream with some manly coughing.

"You are a jumpy thing." Chuckling, he walked up beside her and tilted his head back to take in the heavenly show. "Raney was worried. She thought a bear mighta got ya."

A bear? Grace felt the fear and shock sliding over her face. To hide the gutless reaction, she went back to drinking in this portrait of Heaven, committing it to memory, in case she never had a chance to see it again.

"Bless the Lord, oh my soul," Thad murmured gently, reverently. "Thou art clothed with honor and majesty. Who coverest with light as a garment: Who stretchest out the heavens like a curtain."

Grace tilted her head, impressed. "That was beautiful. Was that Shakespeare?"

He scratched his ear, Grace thought, to hide his surprise at her ignorance. "Uh, no. It's from the Bible."

"Oh." She let her mind wander along the Milky Way, and it led her back to her grandparents' farm. "I used to go to church, back before my parents died."

She could feel him watching her. "You know Shakespeare, but you don't know the Bible?"

"My parents took me when I was very young. My grandparents raised me after their death. My grandfather, though, didn't have much use for religion. He called it superstition."

"What did they do with Grace?"

Grace almost rolled her eyes. Another slip. Panic clawed at her. "They raised us both. She went to church. She went alone." She wished she could swallow the lie—yet another one. Truth be told, she hadn't darkened the door of a church since the flood that took her parents.

"Well, that's good to know." Thad went back to staring at the night sky.

He sounded too pleased. Grace hated to dash his illusions...

"I can't imagine being separated from that."

She didn't follow his thoughts and frowned. "I'm sorry?"

He motioned at the sky. "His love...it's on display up there. This canvas He painted for us. The Bible says the heavens declare His glory. I believe, in Heaven, we're in His presence and it's beautiful and glorious...like that"—he pointed up again—"but beyond anything we can even imagine." He shrugged and folded his arms over his chest. "On the other hand, I believe Hell is knowing everything about God, including how much He loves us, and understanding that you're eternally separated from Him. To *know* that and be alone forever..." He shivered, as if he couldn't imagine anything worse.

Grace thought she had at least a passing acquaintance with that kind of loneliness. A deep, soul-rending isolation.

"Anyway, sorry, don't mean to preach." He slapped her on the back and turned to go. "I'm hittin' the hay. We're all headed to Cheyenne in the morning."

"Cheyenne? The town with telephones?"

Grace's enthusiasm stopped Thad mid-turn. He swung back around to her. "You need to call somebody? Um...Sorry," he waved off the question. "Not that it's any of my business."

With a short pause, he gave her a chance to dispute that. But Grace didn't want to volunteer any information, especially knowing that it would be a lie anyway.

When she didn't offer any details, he nodded. "All right, then, I'll see you tomorrow." He took two steps and stopped. Tugging on his string tie, he rounded on her again. Grace had to consciously restrain herself from begging him to go away, just *leave*.

"Like I said, it's not any of my business, but you can't call Sheridan, if that's what you were thinking. The lines don't run there yet."

"Oh," she said as blandly as possible, hoping to discourage him.

"I mean, if you were thinking about calling your sister, that is..."

That hopeful tone in his voice made her want to throw something at him. This poking around for more information had to stop. "No, I was just thinking what a novelty telephones are. How exciting it would be to talk to someone in, say, Chicago." She shrugged. "Chicago has a lot of telephones."

"And maybe there's a gal back there you might want to give a jingle? Somebody you're sweet on?"

Grace lifted a shoulder. "You could say that."

Thad grunted, seemed to debate something, and then punched her lightly on the shoulder. "You did good, facing Trampas the way you did. Bluffing is half the battle when you're fighting a bigger man." He tilted his head and leaned in a little. "You ever been in a fight?"

Fists flashed before her eyes. Her ribs and back ached at the memory of some of Bull's beatings. "No, not exactly, but I've taken a whooping or two."

Thad chuckled at her honesty. Pondering something, he scratched his nose. "Make a fist."

"What?"

He grabbed her hand and raised it in front of her. "Make a fist."

Scowling and wishing Thad would go on to bed, Grace balled her fingers into a fist and shoved her hand to within an inch of his face. "There."

"Well, that's one reason they were whoopings and not good fights. Here," he clutched her hand, "tuck your thumb in and tighten your fingers." He walked around behind her and raised her other hand. "Same thing, tight fist, and put your feet here and here."

A funny little wiggle flitted around in Grace's stomach as Thad touched her hands, laid a hand on her hip, and his chest brushed her back as he positioned her feet with a nudge of his boot. His warm breath caressed her neck a couple of times as he talked and moved her around.

Satisfied, he slipped around to the front of her again and lifted her hands to just below her eyes. "Keep 'em right there," he stepped back. "Keep your thumbs in, lessin' you want to break them, and throw your punches as hard as you can." He sucked on his cheek, and scanned Grace from top to bottom. "You're awfully spindly. If you're ever in a knock-down-drag-out, Greg, fight with everything you've got. Forget the rules. Go for the vulnerable spots on a man. You take my meaning?"

She slowly lowered her hands, puzzled at his concern—and why she wanted him to continue the lesson. "I think so."

"Good." Dismissing her, he ruffled her hair and jogged back toward the house. "Oh, and you're bunkin' with me for the night," he tossed over his shoulder as he climbed the porch steps. "I'll throw a pillow and a couple of blankets on the floor in front of the fireplace, 'less you want to sleep in the bunkhouse."

The screen door slammed like an exclamation point to Grace's shock.

Chapter Twelve

❦

Thad shoved a blanket and pillow at Grace and gestured to the fireplace. "Make yourself at home."

Grace felt like her tongue was stuck to the roof of her mouth. Then, when Thad sauntered over to his bed and started peeling out of his clothes, the air escaped from her lungs. Realizing she was staring, especially at his rippled stomach, she lunged for the fireplace. She couldn't get the blanket spread fast enough. Trying to make herself small and insignificant, she curled up, facing the fire, and tried to force herself to sleep...on the cold, hard floor.

The sounds of movement and clothes hitting the floor stopped. She flinched, sure he was staring at her.

"You gonna sleep in your clothes?"

Oh, why can't he mind his own business? "Yes."

More silence. A moment later, she heard the door. The quiet told her he'd left the room, but she didn't dare check. She just wanted to curl up here and be left alone. Fully-clothed, no one could tell she was a female. Anything less and the ruse might collapse. She wished Thad slept the same way. He'd peeled down to his long johns and she'd gotten a fine view of his broad chest and lean stomach. She punched her pillow and ordered herself to sleep.

However, a knock at the door foiled that. With the second tap, she rose and answered the caller. Adam stood in the hallway, grinning like he'd just eaten a caged bird. He shoved a pile of clothes at her. "There's a couple of shirts, one pair of jeans, and one pair of long johns that have only been patched once in the rear. Mighty comfortable for sleeping."

"Adam, I can't—"

"Oh, yes, you can. I can spare 'em." He motioned with them and Grace acquiesced, accepting the clothes. "I think they'll be big on ya, but, like my ma used to say, you can grow into them."

"Yes." Grace hesitantly hugged the bundle to her. "Thank you. I'm sure they'll fit...fine." She hoped they'd still be plenty big on her. Adam was much broader through the chest than she was.

"Oh, and hey," he snapped his fingers, "Cheyenne has a new bawdy show. You can go with Nick and me and the boys if you want. I hear some of the gals' costumes are downright racy."

Adam's eagerness to see a burlesque show was both endearing and disappointing. He was a young man trying to grow up in a hurry and eager to find trouble. She noted, though, the name he didn't mention. "What about Thad?"

Adam's face fell. The glee transformed to chagrin.

"Thad doesn't go. And he doesn't approve of us going. Says the show puts us in bad company." The boy's face changed once more. His brow gathered and he set his jaw. "But you got to have some fun sometimes."

"I guess." Grace hated to scold the boy, but Thad was right about the type of men who attended those shows. "There's something else you should consider. Those girls you're gawking at are somebody's daughters. Or sisters. Maybe even mothers."

Adam winced. "Yeah, well..." he scratched his chin. "I guess so. I don't have a sister, so I never thought of it that way."

Grace didn't say anything else. She could see Adam's conscience working on him. He'd go or he wouldn't. She hoped he'd choose the right path and be a better man...like Thad?

"Night, Greg." Dispirited, Adam wandered away down the darkened hallway.

The long johns did look appealing. Grace ran her hand over them as she pushed the door shut with her hip. Soft and freshly-laundered. Did she dare risk changing? She scurried over to the fireplace, glanced over her shoulder at the door once more, and started unbuttoning her shirt.

She was just sliding out of it when Thad knocked and burst into the room. Grace gasped and pulled the shirt back up, grasping it closed in front. "Don't you knock?"

Wearing his long johns unbuttoned to the waist, his lean, upper body exposed, Thad drew up short. He looked so honestly perplexed by the suggestion Grace had to stifle a laugh.

But thinking about what he *could* have seen sobered her.

His bravado returning, Thad sauntered over to his bed. "I don't think you've got anything I haven't seen before."

Wanna bet? "Still, it's polite to knock." She stood with her shirt pinched closed, hugging the long johns like a shield.

Thad scratched his head as if she was an oddity he'd never figure out. "Okay, fine. You like your privacy. How's this?" He leaped onto his bed, slid beneath the covers, and put his back to her.

Grace didn't move for several seconds until she was sure he wasn't *funnin'* her. Convinced, mostly, she faced the fire and finished changing. The long johns were big, but not big enough to hide her curves. She couldn't be seen in them. She wrapped the blanket Thad had given her around herself and settled once again on the floor. Unfortunately, it hadn't softened any in the last few minutes. She punched the pillow, shifted weight off her shoulder, shifted again, and rolled over onto her back.

She surveyed Thad's room, painted in moving shadows from the fire—a bed, a dresser, a desk, and a bookcase filled with books. Over his bed hung a painting of a cowboy standing next to his horse. Because of the dim light, Grace couldn't be sure, but the man sure looked like Thad. Strong jaw, blond hair blowing in the wind, he held the horse's reins in one hand, his hat in the other, and stared off at the distant mountains. His intense, meditative expression gave the picture a sort of melancholy feel, as if he was looking for someone.

"A fella named Charlie Russell did that painting." Thad had rolled back over in the bed and was watching her. "He's gettin' some notoriety now, I hear."

"It's very good. But you look like you're...searching for something."

Thad considered her for a moment then settled on his back. Tucking his hands beneath his head, he studied the ceiling. "Charlie was kind of a sentimental rascal. He said I was lookin' for *her*...a woman...*the* woman."

"Were you?"

"I don't know." He sounded a little frustrated and Grace got the impression he didn't really want to talk about this, yet he continued. "He saw me up on that ridge and rode over. Asked if I'd stay put long enough for him to sketch me in." Thad wagged his foot beneath the covers, showing his agitation. "He asked me the same thing. I said I was lookin' for my future. He said *she* was out there. That God was herding her to Wyoming. Just give Him time."

The strangely sentimental story left Grace puzzled. "You didn't think she was already here?"

His foot stopped. "No, but I think she is now." His expression went from thoughtful to troubled. Grace could see the shadows of the creases on his forehead.

Thinking she should change the subject, she spotted the guitar hiding in the shadows. "Who taught you to play the guitar?"

"We had a hand pass through a few years ago,

Southern boy with a banjo. He sort of helped me figure it out." Thad chuckled softly. "We sure used to have some lively parties here, before Ma died. Back then, Pa even liked the guitar."

"Pardon me for saying so, but he doesn't seem to like much of anything now. Kind of strikes me as a hard case."

"He..." Thad paused here for so long that Grace thought he'd fallen asleep. Then, finally, he said, "Pa is building a future for us, not just for his family, but for his hands and for this state. It's a lot of pressure."

Grace knew an excuse when she heard one, an excuse to cover up a man losing his soul. It wouldn't take much, in her opinion, for Earl Walker to rival Bull in avarice, violence, and ambition. It wasn't her place to say that. It wasn't her place to offer advice, either, but..."You love your pa?"

"Of course I do."

"Then you should talk to him. Try to make him see what he's changing into."

"What makes you such an expert on family?"

"I've seen—" *The darkest side of a man.* "I've seen what Grace is married to. Bull stops at nothing to run his little empire. I mean nothing."

"How did she wind up married to somebody like him?"

Grace took her turn wagging her foot while she thought. *How indeed.* "He's a charmer when he wants to be. But it's just a way he manipulates people. And he moves fast. Pushes them into decisions they're not ready to make." Perhaps if she hadn't been so blinded by the glamour, the charm...

"And she was young," Thad offered. "We make all kinds of mistakes when we're young." Grace knew he was thinking about the stampede again, but there was something else. *Someone* else?

"Yes, all kinds of mistakes," she whispered, the absence of Hardy making her throat hurt.

"Anyway, I was just funnin' you about sleepin' on the floor. Unless you bust broncs in your sleep, you're welcome up here." With that, he rolled over, putting his back on display.

Grace was stunned at the offer. Men sharing beds was certainly a common thing, but she was...well, she was *Grace*.

But he didn't know that.

Her lower back started pounding as the hardwood floor drove into her spine. She eyed the bed...and Thad's outline beneath the quilt. The mattress called to her.

Swallowing her pride—or fear—she rose, went to the bed, and slid in as gently as she could. Her hips and back thanked her. She lay there for a moment, pondering the man next to her, breathing in his scent. He smelled of leather and lilac water. Lying in the bed with him seemed both scandalous and...*comforting*. She flinched at the sordid thought and rolled over onto her side.

But he was so near she could feel the warmth emanating from him.

"Thad, have you ever been with a woman?" The question had leaped unbidden from her mouth, but the way he longed for love, for Grace...intrigued her.

She thought perhaps he didn't know love from physical attraction.

"You mean in the biblical sense?"

The phrase caught her off-guard, but she thought she understood the meaning. "Uh, yes."

"There was a girl a few years back. I thought I wanted to marry her. We almost, but..." Again, he dragged out his response, the long silence full of thoughts Grace wished she could hear. "But I suspected she loved something more than me, and we never..." He shifted in the bed, and the volume of his voice said he had turned toward her. "Since then, I've come to learn the difference."

"The difference?"

"In holding a woman...and holding the *right* woman."

He sounded a little...mystified, as if he were musing out loud. Afraid of intruding but still curious about Thad's observation, she asked, "And you learned that how?"

"Well, my ma told me."

"Your ma? How did she know?"

"She said Pa told her."

Grace had to ponder that. Earl Walker, at one point in his life, had a soft side, a romantic side? She couldn't imagine it.

"Greg, you'll get a lot of pressure from the ranch hands to visit the girls at the Number Nine. Or maybe a girl will come along that you like *a lot,* and it'll be hard to resist..." Thad laid his hand on Grace's shoulder. "But, if you call yourself any kind of a man, wait.

Make sure she's the one you want to spend the rest of your life with. It's the way God intended things."

Grace didn't know what to make of Thad Walker. And, she realized, based on his standards, *she'd* never been with a man. A brute, a bully, a philandering child in a man's body—but not a real man.

Like Thad.

What in the world could a woman love more than him? She frowned, perplexed by the question that he'd so casually glossed over. "What did she love more than you?"

He punched her shoulder and lay back down. "Excitement. Katie wanted to see the world and write about it. One day she will. Right now, she's writing stories for the Cheyenne Daily Sun."

"Did she break your heart?"

Again, he took his time answering. "In hindsight, I guess not. And I'm glad we didn't...you know. That wouldn't have changed the outcome. It would have made things worse." He slapped Greg on the rear end. "So, you make sure you wait. Now get some sleep."

For Grace, though, sleep was a long time coming.

Chapter Thirteen

❧

Cheyenne wasn't much to speak of, Grace thought, surveying the bustling little town, at least not compared to the Windy City, but Raney found numerous things on which to comment. As she and Grace stepped off the train, the older woman scowled at the traffic and shook her head, as if disapproving of the hustle.

"Growin' like a weed. Cheyenne is the capital. You know"—she elbowed Grace in the ribs—"we ain't been a state long."

Grace tossed her saddlebag over her shoulder and thought about an intriguing piece of trivia that had somehow hidden away in her brain. "Didn't Wyoming give women the right to vote?"

Raney puffed up, apparently proud of the forward-thinking state. "We sure did. Only state so far."

The town's main avenue—crowded with horses, riders, wagons, and quick-moving pedestrians—spanned from an impressive brick courthouse down to the stockyards and train station. This area seethed with boisterous cowboys hanging on fences, telling jokes, and tossing ropes. Killing time. Antsy cows mooed and complained in their crowded holding pens. Another train announced its impending arrival with a deafening whistle, and the cowboys moved toward the cattle chutes in one accord.

"Well, it's certainly bigger than Misery." Grace removed her hat and ran a hand through her hair, still surprised by the cropped feel. "I guess that's saying something."

Thad wandered up beside them. "But not as big as Chicago, thank God." He laid a hand on Raney's shoulder. "Pa said let's all check into the Bishop House, get cleaned up, and meet in the lobby for dinner. We'll see ya about five-thirty?"

Raney nodded. "That'll do." She started off in the opposite direction, and Grace followed. "I expect you to behave, young man." She tagged Grace playfully in the ribs. "I'm part owner of the Bishop House. Don't make me look bad."

"You're part owner of a hotel?" Grace didn't really know Raney well enough to judge, but the woman seemed so at home, so content, on the ranch. City life didn't seem to fit the woman at all.

Raney shrugged her shoulders. "Was a time I thought I might let the ranch go. Or at least I thought about retiring here." She surveyed the beehive of a town and pulled her face into a scowl. "Grief. You make bad decisions when you're grieving."

Grace stepped onto the front porch of the Bishop House and tugged her hat lower against a cold gust of wind. Long shadows reached across the nearly empty street, throwing the buildings across the way into early dusk. The lights from the grocer's, butcher shop, and a lawyer's office glowed invitingly.

Evening had quieted this part of town substantially, but Grace could hear the saloons on the next street over—coarse laughter, feminine giggling, pianos, and banjos. The sounds floated to her on the breeze. She flipped up her collar and pulled her coat closer.

Now, where was a phone in this town?

Looking both ways, she crossed the empty street toward the grocer's. To Grace's delight, a sign on the door announced the arrival of the telephone. Private calls available for a fee. She clutched the doorknob, Hardy's little cherubic face rising in her heart. Oh, to hear his voice...

She froze.

She'd already pondered what to do if Bull was home. Hang up. But if he wasn't, should she truly risk getting Hardy on the phone? What if Hardy told Bull about the call? If she was very, very careful in what she said and how she talked to Hardy...

Resolute, or desperate, she opened the door and stepped inside. A tall, older man wearing round spectacles nodded at her from the counter.

"What can I help you with, sonny?"

Grace paused, then remembered her appearance and wondered when this ruse would be second nature. "Uh, yes, I understand you have a phone. I'd like to call Chicago." She strode over to the counter. "How much will that cost me?"

"Five dollars a minute."

Grace's mouth fell open. The clerk hunched his shoulders. "Sorry, son, I don't set the prices. Owner does."

Grace's mouth moved, but she couldn't work out a sound.

"Here, Leroy." Thad pulled a bill from his wallet and laid it on the counter. "I'll cover a minute." He shoved his wallet back into his breast pocket and grabbed a peppermint stick. "You skip dinner, too?"

Grace shook her head, as much from confusion as pride. So absorbed was she in her dilemma, she hadn't even noticed him standing at the end of the counter. "No. I mean, I can't let you do that. Pay for it."

"I don't mind. I expect you're good for it."

Grace studied the young man before her. Those blue eyes glittering with compassion but a hint of mirth, as well, affected her. How, she wasn't quite sure.

Thad punched Grace in the shoulder. "It ain't charity, kid. It's a loan. But, if you don't want to be in debt to me..."

Grace sucked her cheeks in, debating any further involvement with this man. Why was he so nice? If she set aside her pride, then in the next few minutes, she might hear Hardy's little voice. On that hope, she nodded. "All right, thank you. I will pay you back."

"I know." Thad slid the bill to Leroy, who took it and dropped the payment in his register.

"Right this way, son." He slipped out from behind

the counter and motioned for Grace to follow. "We keep it back here so folks can have some privacy."

After allowing Leroy to walk her through the process and then getting an operator on the line, a scratchy, faint ring filled the earpiece. Grace's heart kicked into a gallop. She checked over her shoulder. Thad bid Leroy goodbye and slipped out the front door. The clerk went back behind the counter.

Another ring.

Grace closed her eyes.

And another...

Come on, come on...If I was a praying woman—

"'Ello?" Marie's thick, French accent, tinny and faint, came through the phone, and Grace nearly fainted. "'Ello? 'Endrick residence."

Grace swallowed and leaned into the mouthpiece. "Hello. Is Mr. Hendrick available?"

"No, I am sorry. 'E is out."

Grace exhaled. "Marie." She calmed herself and spoke again, slowly this time. "Marie, can you bring Hardy to the telephone?"

A long silence worried Grace for a moment that the connection had been lost. Then the girl on the other end lowered her voice. "Mrs. 'Endrick?" She sounded stunned. "Is this you?"

Grace knew she shouldn't confess to anything for her sake and for Marie's. She steadied her voice to sound indifferent. "I was calling for Hardy. Might he come to the phone?"

Another long silence and Grace chewed her lip. She had to stifle a cry when Hardy's little voice came through, puzzled and so far away. "Helloooo...?"

How Grace wanted to hug her son, tell him everything, tell him she missed him, that she loved him so much. But she couldn't alarm him, couldn't let him know it was her, which tore out her heart. "Hello, Hardy." She fought to steady her voice. "How are you?"

"Fine."

"Have you..." Grace blinked back tears and swallowed the knot in her throat. "Have you been to the park? Is there a new swing yet?"

The boy brightened. "Oh, yes, the new swing is in. Nanny Doyle and me go every day..." he faded off as if troubled by something. "Daddy didn't let me go for a thousand days, and then he said I could. And the new swing was there."

Grace smiled at his understanding of time. A hundred days, a thousand days. A mere twenty-three days without her son felt like an eternity. "And how is your daddy?"

"Oh, he's fine." Grace was surprised by the quick, confident answer, admittedly even a little hurt.

"And you, you're fine, too, yes?" she asked again.

This time, he didn't answer so quickly. "I'm all right, but my mommy went on a trip and I miss her." Grace had to clutch the wall to keep from collapsing to the floor. With a herculean effort, she held back the sob that cried for freedom. She could almost hear the wheels whirling in Hardy's head. Through the scratchy connection, he whispered, "Mommy?"

She'd done what she came to do. Hardy was fine. She could live on this call for a while longer. She had to. He couldn't know this was her. Otherwise, Bull might take him away. Focusing on what she was fighting for, Grace sniffled, stood up to the pain slicing through her heart, and shook her head. "Your mommy will be home soon, Hardy. She told me. But you have to keep that a secret. Okay? Can you do that?"

"Yes. I guess so. When will she be home?"

Fighting for every ounce of strength she could muster, Grace slowly hung up the phone.

Chapter Fourteen

✦

B lind with grief, Grace wandered down the street. The sun had slipped behind the distant Big Horn Mountains, and the cold sank in. She ignored the passersby, who glanced at her as she sniffled and wiped her nose with the back of her hand.

She seesawed in her mind between missing Hardy and hating Bull. With each step, though, her fury toward the man spread like a poison in her blood.

This whole situation is his fault. What kind of insufferable monster banishes his wife and takes her child away from her?

All those years of rambling around an empty house while he was out philandering played over and over in her head. Lonely Christmas mornings with no clue where he was. The beatings when things didn't suit him. The pitying glances from the servants. The brave face for Hardy. Trying to be the good wife had only earned her Bull's wrath...and loathing.

And *he* had the gall to keep her son from her?

Livid, Grace stopped at the end of the boardwalk. If it took her from now till the Second Coming, she was going to best Bull Hendrick. She was going to get Hardy back, and Bull would never see them again. She swore it to herself—

A squeal jerked her attention to the end of the dark alley. In the faint light of a window, she could see a man and a woman tussling. Grace heard a slap, and the woman cried out.

"Hey!" she yelled, stepping into the alley. "What's going on down there?"

The couple paused.

"Let her alone or I'm going for the sheriff!" Furious for a different reason now, Grace took a step toward them, and another, her feet driven by rage. *No more...no more!* "I mean it, get away from her!"

The man growled, threw his victim to the ground, and bolted off behind the building. Grace rushed to the woman's aid and helped her to her feet. "Are you all right?"

Taking a deep breath, she straightened up. A slender rivulet of blood trickled from her nostril to her lip. "I'm fine, I'm fine." She brushed off her dress, straightened her sleeves, and then slapped an unexpectedly bold gaze on her rescuer. Raising her chin, she assessed Grace from top to bottom. "Well, I think you're about the scrawniest hero I've ever had." Chuckling, she draped her arm over Grace. Her face, delicate and downright stunning in its beauty, revealed no fear, only resignation. "Here, help me to my dressing room, won't you?"

"Certainly." Grace wrapped an arm around the woman, clutched the hand slung over her shoulder, and walked her around to the back of the building. Fumbling between keeping the woman on her feet and opening the door, Grace managed to get her inside, down the hall, and to a settee in a small room.

Relieved, Grace stepped back. The woman really was quite lovely, with regal features, high cheekbones, dark eyes, and auburn hair twisted in a stylish chignon. She wore a stunning blue satin dress that seemed as out of place in Cheyenne as a camel.

Grace glanced around and realized they were in a dressing room. The gas lights framing a large mirror glowed warmly and cast an inviting amber hue over the room cluttered with trunks and dresses.

"Hand me that mirror, please, and a handkerchief."

The woman's voice, now rather matter of fact, snatched Grace back to the moment. She surveyed the messy vanity, found the items, and passed them to her.

"Thank you." The woman studied herself in the mirror and dabbed at her nose. "Because of you, I believe I can perform tonight."

"You're an actress?"

She took another swipe at the blood on her lip then lowered the mirror to appraise Grace. "So they tell me."

Something about her studious gaze made Grace uncomfortable, or was it the amusement twitching on the woman's lips?

"I'm Susanna Kinsey. And I need a drink."

She rose, marched to the vanity, grabbed a decanter, and then spun and hunted the room with a greedy gaze. "Have a seat." The command sounded like an afterthought, but Grace obliged, taking a stool. Susanna spied a shot glass sitting atop a trunk and snagged it. Bottle and glass in hand, she sat back down on the seat at the vanity and poured a drink. "What you did was very brave. You didn't know if that man might shoot you, beat you, or run away."

Taken aback by that, Grace dropped her gaze to the floor. Things certainly could have ended differently. Hardy could be motherless right now if that brute had had a bit more fight in him. But he had made Grace so mad. Or perhaps he had merely been a substitute for Bull. Either way, the desire to throttle the man had taken over Grace's common sense.

"I couldn't take it," she whispered, still staring at the ground. "They can't keep beating on—" She bit off the thought.

"Us?" The woman raised an eyebrow at Grace's surprise. "Ah, don't worry, your secret is safe with me, kid." She spun in her chair and started rummaging around the vanity.

Grace touched her face, concerned something was too feminine about it. "What secret?"

Susanna found a tin box, opened it and removed a cigarillo. "Honey, there are only two reasons a woman pretends to be a man." She searched again among the dozens of makeup containers and came up with a match. She struck it with her thumb, lit the cigar, then shook the light and tossed it back to the vanity. Exhaling, she again regarded Grace with that studious eye. "You don't strike me as the...*scandalous* type, shall we say? I'd wager you like men as much as I do. So, what's

GRACE BE A LADY

your story?" Susanna leaned back and crossed her legs and arms, waiting.

"I don't know what you mean."

"Honey, I'm in the theater. We're all liars pretending to be someone we're not. I can spot an actor a mile away."

Grace broke. "Is it obvious?"

Susanna threw her head back and laughed. "Hell's bells, it should be. But these hayseeds can't see past what's right in front of 'em." The laughter faded and her expression darkened. "You're hiding from a man."

"Not exactly." And Grace told her story. It burst out of her like a breaking dam, and it felt good to finally share her secret.

Susanna sighed at the end and crushed out the remainder of her cigar. "I owe you, Grace Hendrick." She jutted out her hand and the two women shook. "I'll be in Cheyenne for another few weeks, then Casper, then Sheridan. After that, I go home to Chicago for a break." She pulled a card from the messy vanity and handed it to Grace. "When you get your son, if you need a place to stay, go to that address. If you need a job, I'll get you one."

Grace shook her head, stunned at the woman's generosity. "You just met me. Why would you—"

"Because, for an instant, you put my needs above your own—a total stranger." The actress's gaze drifted off. "My father used to tell me stories about a man who did that for all of us." A deep melancholy laced her voice, but she smiled in spite of it. "No one does that anymore, Grace. Thank you."

Feeling quite full of himself, Bull marched down the sidewalk. He tipped his hat politely at the women, nodded knowingly at the men. He was Bull Hendrick, and he was the King of Chicago. Men feared him, on both sides of the law. Women loved him. His bank accounts runneth over. He had the world by its tail. Almost.

He had no reason to check on Grace, but the woman had never quite let go of a spark of resistance, and that troubled Bull.

His step slowed. If she came back, it wouldn't be good for business. He would appear foolish, weak. If he couldn't control one stubborn female, how could he run the South Side?

So he would keep a check on her.

He brushed a little lint from his houndstooth sleeve and entered the Western Union office. From behind the counter, an old man, as gray as a corpse, removed his thick reading glasses. "Help you, sir?"

"I need to send a telegram."

Moving like rigor mortis had already set in, the old man reached for a pad and pencil. "Yes, sir."

Deciding not to let the slow service or concern over Grace spoil his mood, Bull nodded. "To the sheriff in Misery, WY. STOP. Status of..." He jingled the coins in his pocket. He could dole out less if he could shorten this telegram. "No. Correction. To the sheriff Misery, WY. Family inquiring into status of *G*. Hendrick. Reply promptly." As the man finished writing, Bull fished the payment out of his pocket. "Signed, B. Hendrick."

⁂

With renewed vigor, Grace threw herself into the work at the ranch. Hate could do that—energize the tired, focus the lost. Bull would not have the last laugh. He would not keep her son from her.

"Pull it tighter."

A pinch in her finger brought her back to the business at hand and Raney's steely gaze. The two were running fence on a barren stretch of pasture, and the barbed wire had hooked Grace...again. She refocused and leaned back, trying to hold the wire taut.

Shaking her head, Raney finished driving the horseshoe nail into the post then tossed her hammer to the ground. "Let's eat," she grumbled, heading toward the wagon. Grace sensed the woman was displeased. Handling barbed wire with skill was beyond her. Way beyond her. Grace peeled off her left glove and sighed at the red puncture wounds speckling her palm and fingers. She eyed the fence line. Compared to the strands Thad and his hands had run a few days ago, Grace's attempt to help Raney was loose and drooping.

She would get better. She had to.

Raney tossed her a sandwich wrapped in waxed paper. "Here, let's get some meat on those bones." The woman muttered under her breath, "At least I'm gonna die tryin'."

Unwrapping the sandwich, Grace took a seat in the grass and pondered the last few weeks. Add the barbed wire to her string of—well, not failures, exactly—but Grace hadn't done any chores smoothly yet. Raney did everything as if she was born to ranch. Grace, on the other hand, was clumsy and uncertain, like a new foal. Her string of embarrassments paraded through her head.

She had attempted to move the hogs the other day when a boar swung around and ran her up on the fence. Raney, passing by, shoved an unlit cigarette between her lips, opened the gate, whistled, and the animal jogged into the adjacent pen like a house pet.

Grace had mixed up feeding instructions and nearly foundered a horse. She'd built a fire in Raney's kitchen stove but forgot to open the flue. She'd tripped over Dog the other day, crushing a basket of eggs in the dirt. Most noteworthy of all, she'd set a hot branding iron down on Raney's saddle bag and burned a hole clean through it.

The failures made her head ache and she rubbed her temple. If Raney fired her, Grace could only see one option for employment. The thought stole her appetite and she re-wrapped the sandwich. "I think I'll save this for when I'm a little hungrier."

❧

On the way back to the ranch, Raney diverted from the road onto a skinny path. After only a few yards, Grace saw the reason: two white headstones, surrounded by a wrought-iron fence, peeked above the waving autumn grass.

"I rarely drive by without stopping," Raney said, pulling up the brake. "I used to get out and sit for hours. Now I just stop by for a minute. I guess that's good. Life moves on."

Grace hated to ask whose graves they were and figured if Raney wanted to, she would tell her. She surmised one belonged to Jake. But the other?

"Jake...and my son, Cole. One day, I'll be there beside 'em."

Grace flinched. Raney had lost her husband *and* a son. She couldn't imagine losing Hardy. The pain would be utterly insurmountable. And, yet, here sat Raney, carrying on. Grace's respect for her boss increased exponentially.

"Cole's wife Amanda couldn't take the loss. She headed home to Alabama the day after the stampede. Wasn't even here for the funeral."

Stampede? Surely not. "Did your son work for..."

"Earl?" Raney kept her attention on the graves. "Nah. We'd combined our herds that day to get them over into the basin." A gray strand of hair blew loose from her bun and danced along her cheek. "It wasn't Thad's fault. Things happen. It's called ranching."

Grace studied the woman's profile. A sharp nose and high cheekbones revealed the ghost of a young girl, once pretty, mostly likely full of hope. Now, Raney wore pain and forgiveness in every wrinkle. Hard-fought lines. "I'm sorry."

The woman shrugged and released the brake. "I've still got my daughter Katie. Sort of."

Katie? That Katie?

"She moved away to write for a newspaper. Wants to see the world. She'll go pretty far afield, I expect, but one day, she'll come home to Wyoming."

An inexplicable sense of dismay drove Grace's spirits even lower. "I'm sure she will," she whispered without any enthusiasm.

Chapter Fifteen

❧

Thanks to Thad, Grace had developed at least one skill useful on a ranch. She could drive nails.

Confident she could handle this new project, she climbed a ladder and emerged on the line shack's roof. The view stopped her in her tracks. Rolling plains, the rich amber of honey, dipped and rose toward the towering, snow-capped Big Horn Mountains. Blond cottonwoods lined the creek, revealing its meandering path through the valley. A mile away, Raney's white farmhouse and red buildings glowed against the shimmering sea of tawny grass. Sunshine peeked intermittently through rolling gray clouds but didn't deliver any warmth.

Grace liked Wyoming. Lonely, quiet, filled with wild animals and vast, empty distances, as opposite of Chicago as the South Pole...yet she felt peace here. A place she could call home.

The November breeze tossed occasional

snowflakes about as it carried along the contented mooing of the herd, reminding her of the job she'd come to do. Cedar shingles covered the swaybacked roof before her, but several were missing in the center near the crumbling, river rock chimney. Two more trips up the ladder, and she had her supply of nails and shingles at the ready. The roof, though, was fairly steep, and several times, one or the other of her supplies tried to slide off. Frustrated, she laid shingles atop the chimney, hooked the nail bucket over her arm, dropped to her knees, and slid a plank into place. Pulling the hammer from her belt, she went to work.

More than once, shingles shifted out from under her, adding several more to the number to be replaced. Undaunted, she worked hard and at a steady pace. Finally, down to the last repair, she crept toward the chimney like she was walking on eggs and grabbed a shingle. She stepped over a few feet and squatted to nail it in place.

The cedar beneath her right foot let go with a screech. Grace's weight shifted, and her feet slipped out from under her, throwing her face down onto the roof. She rocketed feet-first toward the edge, clawing and scrambling like a madman for something stationary. More shingles ripped loose beneath her fingers, and Grace went over the ledge in a shower of cedar.

The fall wasn't all that far, and she tried to right herself before hitting the ground, but her left foot landed on a rock and slipped sideways. White-hot pain seared deep into her ankle and shot up her leg. She howled and collapsed hard on her rear end. Tears sprang to her eyes. Moaning, she commenced rubbing the burning ankle furiously, trying to snuff out the breath-taking pain. She writhed in torment, swinging her head back and forth and panting like a dog.

"Holy cow, you're lucky you didn't break your neck."

Pounding hoof beats barely cut through the black shroud of pain that surrounded her like a fog. She recognized Thad's voice but couldn't let go of the agony consuming her. Oh, God, when would it stop?

"Here." Thad moved her hands. "Let me make sure it ain't broke."

Grace had the urge to punch him for butting in, but it was fleeting. At his touch, the pain started slowly ebbing to something that didn't make her want to throw up. Thinking a bit more clearly, she watched Thad's hands with fascination as he carefully worked the boot off her foot, then the sock, and ran warm fingers lightly over the ankle.

"Hmmm. Hard to tell yet. You sure got little bones. Did you hear anything snap?"

He cupped his hands around her ankle and heel. She was amazed at how good his touch felt, like a balm to her injury, and she found herself wishing he'd keep holding her that way.

"No, it just felt like a wrenching."

He pulled away. "All right, let's see if you can put any weight on it." He hauled her to her feet. Grace made the effort, but any weight at all sent pain exploding from the ankle in all directions. She gasped and folded, but Thad caught her before she collapsed to the ground. "Guess that answers that. Let's get you back to Raney's." He retrieved his horse and positioned it next to Grace. Taking a breath, he lifted her into the saddle, sideways. "Shoot, you don't weigh anything, boy."

He rolled her sock gently back up on her foot, handed her the boot, then stepped into the stirrup and settled in behind her. The warmth coming off his chest made butterflies flutter in her stomach. A little unnerved by her reaction, she pulled away, but realized quickly that was no way to ride.

"What about the wagon?"

"I'll come back for it. Here," he pulled her to him, "lean on me and rest your foot over Bo's neck."

Settled, Thad kicked his horse into an easy lope. Grace closed her eyes and pretended for a moment the man holding her was all hers—his strong arms, his warm body, his hips moving rhythmically with the horse. She could so easily drift and dream about his lips brushing her neck...

"You even smell like her."

Reality fell on Grace like a brick, and she moved away from him, just enough so she wasn't touching him. What had she heard in his voice? Longing?

"Greg, I'll give you a hundred dollars if you get your sister to the dance."

"That all she's worth?" Grace tried to sound offended but didn't think she quite accomplished it.

"Name your price," Thad responded instantly. "Then double it. And, in truth, it still wouldn't be enough."

In spite of her throbbing ankle, a smile deviled the corners of Grace's mouth.

Grace let Raney guide the injured foot into a bowl of water so cold it felt like thousands of needles stabbing her skin. She gasped and then gasped again as the water magnified the blue skin and copious swelling.

Drying her hands on her skirt, Raney rose and stepped back to lean on the kitchen counter with Thad. "I think it's just a sprain, but you'll be off your feet for a few days."

Grace sagged. Ranching was proving to be a daily exercise in disaster. "I'm sorry, Raney. I must be the worst hand you've ever had." Miserable, she pondered her foot, and cursed that stupid shingle. If she didn't get a handle on this job, Raney was going to go looking for a new hand, and then where would she be?

At the Number Nine.

"No. No, you're not the worst," she dead-panned. "I had one fella burn down the outhouse. *That* was mighty inconvenient." The hint of compassion in Raney's voice brought Grace's head up. The old woman was smiling and mischief danced in her wise, brown eyes. "'Least you ain't set nothin' on fire. And I still think you'll be able to dance a song or two at the Christmas social."

"Yeah, about that..." Thad dragged a chair out from the kitchen table and straddled it so he could face Grace.

The eagerness in his expression, like a man waiting to escort his gal on their first outing, made her want to sigh, but she held it back.

"The social is in Sheridan. We all go. I was serious

about you rounding up your sister. Think you can bring her?"

"No," Grace snapped, crossing her arms over her chest. "I told you, she's got enough trouble right now without adding a cow*boy* into the mix."

Thad waved his finger at Grace and rose to his feet. "You need to quit calling me that, Buttercup. *I* would never, ever strike a woman."

Grace saw his gaze skip quickly to Raney. So she had filled in some of the details about Bull. He leaned toward her an inch. "Now, you, on the other hand—"

Grace ignored the threat. "Snake or not, she's *married* to him."

The observation drew him up short, but only for an instant. Thad didn't exactly storm out, but he marched off without any goodbyes. Grace stared at the door for a few moments, puzzled that she found herself wishing he hadn't left, especially in a huff. In the background, Raney banged around in the kitchen, working on dinner.

"I've never seen him like this. 'Specially over a girl." Shaking her head over the mystery, she pulled a frying pan from the back of the stove to the front burner. "Your sister's husband. Has he been *unfaithful* to her too?"

"Marriage didn't change anything about Bull's ways. He just dropped the lies after we—I mean, *he*—and Grace were hitched. He drinks, he runs around on her."

Scowling, Raney cut a chunk off the ham hanging overhead. "A man like that oughta be horsewhipped. They got children?"

Grace wanted to scream at Raney to stop the inquisition. To that end, she changed the topic. "No, ma'am. Here," she rose to her feet and shook the water off the swollen ankle, "let me help with dinner. At least I can do that."

"You sit right back down, I'll bring you some potatoes to peel."

As Grace worked at the task, her mind wandered back to Thad. His hands, firm but gentle on her ankle, had made her heart beat faster, surprising her. His vehement reaction to being compared to Bull had surprised her, as well. In a flight of fancy, Grace wondered if maybe Thad was different. Maybe he wouldn't have a wife merely for the illusion of respectability. Maybe he wouldn't beat her if she asked where he'd spent his evening. Maybe he could say nice things to her, and mean them.

Then again, she'd never once suspected Bull's dark side until they were married. Every man had one. Even Thad Walker.

Thad rode his horse away from Raney's at a full gallop but got control of himself a half mile out. Disgusted that he was acting like a child, he slowed Bo to a walk. He shouldn't let Greg get to him like that. After all, he was right. Grace had no room for someone else in her life. Biblically speaking, Thad was out of line even thinking about her. She was married, for Pete's sake, regardless of *what* she'd married.

Lord, forgive me. He reined his horse to a stop and

snatched his hat from his head. He scanned the big, open expanse of the Powder River Basin. The wind drifted across the cut hayfield like a moaning ghost. Blue, snow-tipped mountains reached for the gray sky roiling with clouds.

Nowhere to hide...from himself or God.

I'm sorry, Lord. I don't know why I'm so drawn to her. Forgive me.

He replaced his hat and sighed.

"I know I should pray that her husband will give his heart to You and repent of his evil ways. I know I should ask You to remove this attraction I have for Grace," he exhaled like an exasperated horse, "but what I want to pray is that You'll remove Bull...by any means. Guess You've still got some work to do in me."

Wishing he were a more noble man, Thad kicked Bo and they headed home.

Chapter Sixteen

❦

G race was sure she was going to be sick. Wedged in among Thad and half-a-dozen hands from the Lazy H, she marched with the men down a Sheridan boardwalk toward the Western Hotel. Dressed in clean shirts and dungarees, their spurs a-jingling, the cowboys' walk had a definite swagger to it as they anticipated the dance. At least she had again managed to get out of bunking with these boys, but she hadn't figured out how to get out of attending the social.

"Buttercup there just might get his first kiss at the dance, Thad," Jay smooshed Grace's hat down over her head and laughed, "if there's anybody there his size."

The other cowboys laughed, and Grace felt the heat rush to her cheeks as she righted the hat.

Jay persisted in the teasing, "Have you ever been kissed, Buttercup?" Delighted with his target, he pinched Grace's neck. "Come on, spill, Buttercup."

Grace slapped Jay's hand away, but as she spun on

the bobbing Adam's apple, Thad pressed the back of his hand to Jay's chest. "That's enough."

Knowing she had to stand her ground or endure more of this torment, she stopped in front of Jay, blocking his path. Startled for an instant, a wide, easy grin quickly lifted the corners of his mouth. "Just yuckin' it up with ya, greenhorn. No offense meant."

Grace thought about the best way to respond. Beside Jay, Thad chuckled and pushed his hat back an inch. "Jay, Buttercup there just might prove to be as mean as a little badger. If I were you, I'd cut him some slack."

Grace pursed her lips, gave Jay as dark a glare as she could muster, then spun on her heel and marched down the boardwalk. The ranch hands laughed off the incident and moved on. They followed behind her, discussing the fine food usually served at the dance.

Grace tried to ignore them, instead focusing on the bustling town and the sounds around her. The laughter, the jingle of wagons—

She saw the tin star sauntering toward her, and her steps faltered.

"Outta the way, you bunch of yahoos."

Grace snatched her hat lower and peered into a store window as the sheriff shoved her aside. He pushed through the Lazy H men, paused as he came to Thad, but then tipped his hat. Thad touched the brim of his hat and offered a friendly, but not enthusiastic, nod and then cut his eyes quickly to Grace as the sheriff strolled on by. Had Thad seen her attempt to evade the sheriff? Afraid of potential questions, she stepped up her pace to put some distance between herself and the boys.

There was only one sheriff she should worry about, and he most likely would not recognize her. After all, she looked nothing like the young lady in the lovely blue dress.

Lost in her own thoughts, Grace nearly walked into the swirl of red taffeta. "Oh, pardon me—"

Susanna Kinsey.

Escorted by a tall, muscular man in an expensive suit, Susanna clutched his arm and pulled back, but then recognition lit her face. Before she could greet Grace, though, the horde of cowboys surrounded the actress and started talking all at once...all of them except Thad.

"Miss Kinsey, you are fetching tonight."

"I saw you in Dodge City. Best play I ever saw."

"Will you be joining us at the dance tonight?"

The bodyguard with her took a step forward, and the cowboys backed off. Susanna extended her hand to Grace. "Maxwell, this is my pint-sized hero I was telling you about."

The man nodded knowingly at Grace. She would have been offended by the betrayal, but Susanna stepped over and took her by the arm. "So, you're attending a dance this evening, are you? Won't that be lovely?" She started pulling Grace away from the gawking cowboys. "First, you must let me repay you for your chivalry and daring-do. I would just adore having a drink with the handsome young man who saved me from a ruffian."

The hands from the Lazy H, including Thad, stared like little boys at their first burlesque show.

Susanna giggled wickedly. "Don't worry, fellows, I'll get him to the ball on time."

"I can't do this, Susanna. I don't even want to go to this dance."

Susanna huffed and sagged with the stunning violet silk and toile gown in her arms. "Grace, pretend you're Cinderella. Take one evening to enjoy life. To be the beautiful belle of the ball. To drop those men to their knees and make them worship you." She stepped closer and searched Grace's face. "I can make you beautiful. More beautiful than Bull could ever imagine...or ever deserve."

Grace had to admit she liked that idea. She would love to swirl and dance and send the men swooning. Bull had not allowed her to go to the theater or restaurants without him, and he rarely took her with him. Neither did she attend parties outside their home. Grace was swallowed up by Bull's dark, cold world. No wonder Seth had managed to tempt her. She'd been starved for affection, but also for having her femininity...cherished.

"What will you do about my hair?"

Susanna licked her plump, red lips and smirked like Satan's mistress. "Oh, I've got a trick or two up my sleeve."

"Those independents have got to understand this is *our* range."

Fred Hesse's nasally, English accent grated on Thad's nerves. No, that wasn't the whole truth, the conversation was also more than a little annoying. Anytime there was an audience, Hesse harped on the SGA's *right* to run the range, like they were gods sitting on Mt. Olympus.

Trying to ignore the man, Thad surveyed the buffet. Shrimp, oysters, juicy roasts, and a plethora of steamed vegetables and decadent desserts testified to the money and power of the Wyoming Stock Growers Association.

At the end of the banquet table, a group of the prominent cattle barons, including his father, were having a go at their favorite pastime: blaming the independents for all the troubles in the state.

"They've big ideas of money and grandeur when all they're doing is destroying the grazing potential of some fine parcels," Hesse ranted on, "and they've the gall to steal our cattle to do it."

Thad thought back to Sheriff Angus's observation that the big outfits were creating cover for something. Either he was lying, or they were lying. If the cattle barons were telling the truth, then why did they feel the need to pay the newspapers?

Lord Morton Frewen nodded absently at Thad over the buffet, and picked up an hors d'oeuvres. "Agreed, Mr. Hesse. *We* know what's best for this land."

"We've the money and resources to make Wyoming the cattle capital of the world," Major Frank

Wolcott chimed in from the group at the end of the table. "This rustling must be stopped so we can get on with things. I feel we've been too gentle with these ne'er-do-wells. Bothwell was right all along."

Thad swung his head up. Bothwell had spearheaded Ella Watson's lynching. The lynching of a woman. He opened his mouth to argue, but his pa spoke first.

"What Bothwell did to Ella was not acceptable, and he'll pay for that in the fires of hell. You don't lynch a woman. You don't murder a woman." Earl tossed back the whiskey in his hand. "Now, the men, on the other hand, far as I'm concerned, we've given them all fair warning."

A shrimp slipped from Thad's fingers as his appetite vanished. When had Earl Walker ever agreed with vigilante justice?

Thad studied the group of wealthy, tuxedo-clad aristocrats over which his father towered like a great oak—lords, Harvard graduates, military men who thought the land belonged to them along with everything on it. Not one man in that group had fought and bled for his range the way Pa had. Not one of them had personally tangled with Indians or rustlers.

Pa had always respected the right of any man to come to this country and give ranching a try. And he'd never been one to fall in with a herd. Ever. He led, or he didn't go at all.

Admittedly, though, Thad had sensed a change in his father over the last few years.

More and more settlers moved into Wyoming every day. Just like Pa had done in '62, these men came here to build their dreams, discover their destinies. Seemed the way of things to Thad, but Pa had been grumbling more and more about it lately.

Thad despised admitting it, but tonight, Pa, in his tailored tuxedo and custom-made boots, didn't look a whole lot different from the preening peacocks at his elbows.

Disturbed by his father's change of heart, Thad moved away from the cattle barons and joined his men over at the bar. Trampas was in the group but kept to himself at the far end.

Thad didn't drink much, but he preferred the conversation of honest, hardworking, whiskey-swilling ranch hands to those coyotes in black ties. He dipped himself a cup of punch and watched the swirling, waltzing crowd. There was a lot of money in this room tonight, and a lot of pretty gals, to boot. None of them was as pretty as—

Grace Hendrick stood at the top of the three stairs leading to the dance floor, and Thad's breath caught in his chest.

Chapter Seventeen

✦❧❧✦

T had'd heard the expression *thunderstruck* before, but until he saw Grace there, he'd never grasped the meaning.

The gaily-lit room filled with a hundred people faded away. The boisterous cattlemen and their ladies in shimmering evening gowns disappeared. The jaunty fiddles and banjos fell silent. Thad's world consisted only of Grace in a violet silk gown that hugged her feminine curves and lit her jade eyes. Her silky, strawberry-gold hair was swept up and pinned in place with a matching ostrich feather, but a group of delicate curls hung loose and rested over one smooth, bare shoulder. Her shoulders, throat, décolletage—each begged for his touch.

Snapping his mouth shut, he gulped out of shock and...yearning. He downright hungered to be close to her.

"Holy smokes, is that the girl from town?"

Adam's elbow to Thad's ribs brought back the

noisy ballroom, the music...and the other cowhands gawking at Grace.

"'Scuse me." Thad shoved his cup of punch into Adam's hands and marched toward Grace. Their eyes met as he crossed the dance floor, and hers widened a bit. Other than that change in expression, he couldn't hazard a guess as to what she was thinking...which didn't encourage him.

Still, he couldn't stop himself. She drew him like the proverbial moth to the flame.

Lord, just one dance and I'll step away.

He stuck out his hand. "Ma'am, you might not remember me—"

"Thad Walker." She smirked. Staring at his hand, she hesitated an instant before shaking it.

He held her small, gloved hand in his and determined he wouldn't let it go. At least, not for a while.

"You remember me." He contemplated her eyes, wondering at the flecks of blue amid the green. Grace licked her lips and pulled her hand away, lacing her fingers behind her back. Thad knew he needed to speak. Thoughts wouldn't form.

"Thad Walker, you're wasting this young lady's time."

Tall and straight, chest puffed out like a rooster's, Trampas extended his hand to Grace. "I'm sure she'd much rather dance with me." His smug expression made Thad want to stomp the cockiness right out of the foreman, except that he saw the change in Grace. Her brow creased ever-so-slightly and her chin lifted a hair.

"Actually, Mr. Walker just asked me for this dance.

But thank you." There was no warmth in her voice and Thad puffed up a bit himself.

Trampas dropped his hand. "Then I'll come back around in a bit, ma'am." He shot Thad a venomous look and departed in the direction of the bar.

Grace gave her hand to Thad, and they stepped into the waltz. Her small waist beneath his fingers felt like the most natural place his hand had ever rested. Though her face was unreadable, she held his gaze.

Those eyes of hers...

He couldn't stop thinking that. Clear and green like a mountain lake, they just about knocked the wind out of him.

They danced for a moment without words. Thad needed the time to pull his head out of the clouds. Grace was intoxicating. She fogged his brain like too much liquor.

He chuckled at the comparison, and she tilted her head. "Did I say something funny, Mr. Walker?"

"No, ma'am, I was reflecting on how you...on how you..." *Take my breath away.* He trailed off and cleared his throat.

"On how I...dance?"

"Not exactly." Thad eyed the chandeliers burning brightly overhead and wondered why he was suddenly as eloquent with this woman as a drunk cowhand on a Saturday night. "I mean, you do dance wonderfully." Thad risked a glance down and found himself mesmerized by full, sweet lips, a long, graceful neck, soft shoulders, and—he snatched his gaze back to her face. A drowning sensation rose up in him, but not like he was dying. Quite the opposite. "You could tear a man slap out of the saddle."

She arched her brow. "I'm sorry?"

Oh, for the love of... He flinched at his foolish tongue.

"My brother gave you too much credit, Mr. Walker. He said he you were a silver-tongued, puffed-up cowboy who dallied with women for fun. I wonder if he was speaking of one of your brothers."

Thad's jaw tightened. *I'm gonna kill that kid.*

"He's got it all wrong, ma'am. I've never toyed with a woman's affections." He regarded her with intensity, hoping the truth of that was evident. "Unfortunately, the reverse is not true."

She looked away, losing a little of her fight.

"Is your brother here? Did he escort you?" *Can I take him out back and beat him?*

"No." Grace paused here, overly long, Thad thought. "He was going to dine with a friend and then come to the dance."

"Was that friend the actress lady?"

Grace nodded. "Uh-huh."

"Greg neglected to tell us how he came to be acquainted with her. She plucked him from our group as we were heading toward the hotel. I nearly stopped her, as I think she's racy company for a young boy, but then I decided it wasn't any of my business."

The dance ended and the room of revelers applauded. Thad spotted Trampas making his way toward Grace again. "Another dance? You'd best say yes unless you want to twirl with the likes of him."

Grace frowned. "I don't like him. He reminds me of...someone."

Thad could guess who that someone was. Wishing he could whirl Grace away from Trampas *and* her husband, he eagerly slid his arm around her once again. He pulled her in among the dancers, but not before he saw the thundercloud on Trampas's face. Reveling in his foreman's defeat, Thad winked at him.

"Why don't you think the actress is good company for Greg?" Grace asked as Thad twirled her around. He might be tongue-tied, but he could at least waltz with some skill.

"She looked at him strangely, like she had a devil of a plan in mind for him. And Greg is an innocent boy. Innocence should be protected." Grace fell quiet, but Thad could see the thought captured her attention. He'd like to protect her, too, even though it wasn't his place.

He reminded himself they were at a party and attempted to lighten the mood. "What do you enjoy doing, Mrs. Hendrick? Do you have any interests?"

"I was in teaching school for a while. I believe I will go back to that, as circumstances allow."

Sadness flitted across her face as they box-stepped and spun. He couldn't help but ask, "Why did you leave it?"

"I'd rather not talk about me, if you don't mind."

"My apologies, I didn't mean to be nosy. It's just that Greg, well, he doesn't say much, just enough to let me know you've had trouble with your husband."

The comment seemed to push her away. She looked here and there, at the guests, at the lights, everywhere but at him.

He decided a drink might be in order.

"It's chilly outside. Would you like to rest a moment in the library and have a little champagne? I don't usually drink, but I could do with a glass. It is a party, after all."

"You don't drink?"

"I've got no use for liquor, ma'am, but I will enjoy a beer or glass of wine...if the company suits."

Chapter Eighteen

❦

Grace settled on a settee in the library, in front of a roaring fire, and marveled over this strange sense of...contentment. She felt so pretty and admired. Susanna had done a masterful job of styling the wig. It matched Grace's hair to a T. And the dress, from the House of Wirth, was one of the most beautiful creations she had ever worn.

A sleeveless gown with a fishtail skirt, its flowing tulle embroidered with birds and roses, floated like gossamer. The bodice, adorned with the same intricate embroidery, was a bit too low for Grace's taste. She smiled, recalling that while Trampas had directed his comments more at her bosom than her face, Thad had tried averting his eyes.

Absently rubbing her sore ankle, she wondered if he could be that much of a gentleman? *And* a virgin?

"Here you go, m'lady."

Grace accepted the glass as Thad joined her on the

couch. Again, he whipped his eyes away from her neckline. Avoiding temptation, or being gentlemanly?

"Feet sore already?" He glanced at her boots.

"No, I twisted my ank...le." She faded off, alarmed she'd let that slip.

He sat. "Funny. Your brother fell off a roof and twisted his ankle."

"Yes, he mentioned that." Grace tried to hide behind the glass as she took a sip.

Thad shifted on the settee to face her and leaned forward, resting his arms on his knees. His eager gaze made her feel as though she was the most important thing in his world, at least at this moment.

"Where did you wind up finding work here in Sheridan?" he asked.

"Work?" She should have expected this question and kicked herself for not being prepared.

"Yeah, Greg said you found something in town." He wiggled his eyebrows comically. "Bunkhouse cook maybe?"

They both laughed. "No...I'm waiting on tables at...at..." She wanted to pound her head. She hadn't paid attention to any of the business names in town.

"Dolly's Café?"

"Yes, that's it. I'm so new I forgot the name. What about you?" She changed the subject. "What is life like for the son of a cattle baron?"

"I'm sorry." He dipped his head in apology. "You said you didn't want to talk about yourself."

He leaned back on the settee's arm. The light from the fire shimmered in his hair and gave the landscape of his face an almost devilish edge, but nothing sinister like Bull. Grace decided she could sit here and stare at that face all night.

"Ranching." He drummed his fingers on the champagne flute. "The work is hard, the days are long, the money is uncertain, and the help more trouble than they're worth," he glanced over her shoulder, perhaps thinking of Trampas in the other room, "but, truthfully, there's nothin' I'd rather do."

Grace liked the way his expression softened as he talked about ranching. She liked the way his white silk shirt tightened across his shoulder and bicep as he took a sip of the champagne. She liked him better riding tall in the saddle, blue eyes scanning the hills, a powerful horse willingly under his command. "You were born to it."

"Yes, ma'am. I find peace in the saddle, looking up at the sky, enjoying the wide-open spaces. And it's a family business. I work close with my brothers and I ain't ashamed to admit I'm pretty fond of 'em."

They laughed together at that.

"I went to Chicago once, though. I couldn't believe the miles and miles of buildings." He shivered dramatically. "It ain't for me. Don't know how people can live like that."

Thad's honesty and deep, velvety voice spurred her to talk about herself, just a little. "I would say you get used to it, but that's not true. At least it wasn't for me. Raised on a farm, I never got used to being surrounded by brick and concrete."

"May I ask again about your becoming a teacher?" He sounded so gentle and hesitant, Grace almost laughed. Almost.

"I was a teaching student in Chicago. I met Bull, and he overwhelmed me with flowers, romantic dinners, and midnight carriage rides..." Grace trailed off, humiliated by her shallowness. "All just so I'd marry him, for nothing but a charade."

Thad's brow dipped, questioning. She'd started the story, might as well finish it. "He needed a respectable wife. One who could help create the illusion that he was a respectable businessman."

The music in the other room slowed to a romantic waltz, and Grace almost wished they were dancing again. Thad's arm around her waist had felt...comforting, and electrifying at the same time.

Thad sat up and rested an arm on the back of the settee. The move drew him closer. His gaze drifted to her mouth, and her heart started racing. How easily he could kiss her, if she'd let him, if he were so inclined. He swirled the champagne around in the glass as he thought. "Pa's done all the hard work building the Lazy H, but we'll keep it going. My children and their children and their children's children will be raising cattle in Wyoming for a long time to come."

He looked at her then. Silence settled between them, but not an awkward kind. Thad's eyes glowed, warm and inviting. Grace had never seen such tenderness. She felt...*undone* by it.

"I sure would like to dance with you again, Mrs. Hendrick."

Pretend you're Cinderella. Take one evening to enjoy life. Grace could hear the words so clearly, and she longed for the fairy tale.

What could one more dance hurt?

She took their glasses of champagne and set them on the end table. Then she turned back to Thad, surprised at the butterflies dancing in her stomach. "Lead the way."

"Right here is fine."

He pulled her to her feet and slid an arm around her. Drawing her close to him, he clutched her hand to his chest. Grace had the nearly overwhelming desire to touch his face, trace the strong, clean-shaven jaw, and move one unruly strand of blond hair out of his eyes.

The music played, yet he made no move to lead her into a dance. His eyes burned into hers, and she felt like she was staring into the sun. He splayed her hand out atop his heart and, with his other hand, touched her jaw, tilting her face up.

Her own heart pounded like a hundred thundering hooves. Merely breathing became difficult, and her head swam. Beneath her fingers, his heart hammered wildly, and he smiled at the silent communication.

"What have you done to me?" He sounded... pleased.

He leaned down and brushed her lips. Grace didn't move, couldn't think. She could only feel the softness of his mouth, the tightening of his arm around her, the gentle caress of his fingers on her cheek.

But, abruptly, he pulled back.

The regret on his face broke her heart and sobered her.

"I said I don't dally with women." He let her go and stepped away a respectable distance. "If I can't have you, I reckon that's what this is." He swallowed hard. "My apologies."

Humiliation and disappointment stung Grace hard. She chided herself for coming tonight. What had she been thinking to let Susanna talk her into this? Of course, he was right.

She swept up her skirt. "Excuse me. I think I see my brother."

Mortified, she ran from the dance, from Thad, and from her foolish heart.

Chapter Nineteen

❧

Grace snatched her cloak from the hallway rack and raced back to the theater. The backstage doorman had been told to let her in, and she scurried past him to Susanna's dressing room.

The woman was still on stage, and Grace collapsed onto her settee. She felt on the verge of tears but couldn't rightly say why. Her heart and her thoughts racing, she rose and went to Susanna's mirror.

Grace took one last look at the arguably pretty young lady, her cheeks glowing, her eyes shining. Biting her lip to hold back a whimper, she raised her hands to the wig and slowly began the dismal process of changing back into Greg.

❧

In a little while, applause erupted. Moments later, Susanna bounced into the dressing room with a bouquet of red roses that matched her velvet gown exactly. Maxwell shut the door behind her and faced the hoard of admirers outside.

"Hello, Cinderella," Susanna sang gaily as she tossed the roses onto a chair. "The clock has struck midnight and you're an ash girl again, eh?" Laughing, she poured herself a drink and faced Grace. Almost instantly, the joy from a well-received performance melted off her face as she noticed Grace's mood. She joined her on the settee and took her hand. "You look like you've come from a funeral, not a party. What in the world went wrong?"

"I'm not really sure," Grace exhaled. "I only danced a few times with Thad Walker. But, it was...he was..." She shook that off. "I don't know. I should never have gone. It was a terrible idea." Grace's throat tightened and she fell against the settee's arm. The feel of Thad's arms haunted her. His voice filled her ears. She felt despicable for lying to him. Oh, why was she being so emotional about this? Later tonight or tomorrow, she would see Thad, but he would see only Greg. He could never see Grace again. End of story.

Sniffing, she sat up again. "I...I'm just tired. I've taken on a lot. This ruse is difficult to keep up." She wiped her eyes and patted her cheeks to freshen their color. "I'm being silly."

"You're a woman, and women were made to be admired, to occasionally turn heads...and to fall in love," Susanna said gently. "Did you not enjoy being in his arms?"

Involuntarily, Grace sighed and relived the

moment he'd held her and kissed her. A warm blush spread over her, and Susanna laughed again.

"Oh, my, he must be something. If only you could see your face." She rose and went to her vanity. In another minute, she had a cigar burning and studied Grace through a smoky haze. "Well? Who is this handsome prince?"

"His family owns the Lazy H. He helps the widow woman I work for. Ooooh," Grace moaned, diving back for the settee's arm to hide her face. "And I'm telling him such a terrible lie. And her. I've got to get back to Chicago. I've got to get my son. And I've got to quit lying to them."

"There's nothing wrong with a *good* lie, Grace. Your intentions are noble."

"My intentions...are for my son." Grace bit her lip and shook her head. "It doesn't feel like a good lie anymore. It just feels deceitful. Plain and simple."

❧

Thad stormed into his suite, snatching his tie off like it was a snake around his neck. Kicking the door shut behind him, he threw the black ribbon across the room and stomped over to the fireplace.

"Well, somebody didn't finish the evening on a good note."

Startled, Thad spun and discovered his father and Trampas standing at the bar. "Sorry, Pa, I..." Bitterness rose up in him at the sight of the foreman, but he swallowed it. "I didn't know you were here."

Thad rested his elbows on the fireplace mantle

and listened to the clink of glass as his father poured a drink. He dreaded the lecture that was coming. Thad couldn't do anything right, not even walk away from a married woman, which surely had to be the right thing to do. And Trampas was here to enjoy the misery.

"Well, I reckon I'll be heading out to catch up with the boys." A chink followed Trampas's declaration. "Thank you for the drink, Mr. Walker."

"Good night, Trampas."

Thad heard Trampas let himself out as Pa shuffled over to the settee. An instant later, he dropped his boots on the coffee table with a thud. "So what's got you so riled? That little filly you were dancing with?"

Yes, Thad was upset over how the evening had ended with Grace, but he was none too pleased with how it had started. Now, to find Trampas in here with his pa, why did he feel like the two of them were keeping secrets? The way Pa tolerated and defended the man just didn't make any sense. "Tell me some-thin', Pa, you really siding with those lying, back-shooting, woman-lynching cattlemen?"

The fire popped and hissed as Thad waited for an answer. Surprised when one didn't come, he turned to his father.

Pa stared gloomily at his boots. "In for a penny, son, in for a pound."

"What?"

Pa tossed the drink back and rose to pour another. He seemed agitated, distant. Thad hadn't seen his father like this in a long time. Not since the year Ma had died and Raney's husband Jake was killed. That year, death seemed to stalk the Walkers and those closest to them.

"The rustlers, they're out of hand, Thad. They've gone too far. We have to end this before any more innocent people die."

"Those are lies." Thad crossed the room and pulled his father around to face him. "I talked to Sheriff Angus. *Five* cases, Pa, *five* of cattle rustling and horse-stealing."

Pa's face reddened, the warning of an explosion. "The independents are stealing our cattle!"

"If anybody is stealing anything, it's Trampas!"

Pa's mouth snapped shut. Thad had wanted proof before voicing that accusation, but he couldn't take it back now. "I couldn't figure it out at first. Now I understand. The big outfits are *using* the newspapers and their political connections to shut the independents down. It's all lies. You're painting them as thieves, bandits, and liars so the conglomerates come off as the victims." Thad lowered his head and dropped his hands on his hips as he walked away to think. "But I still don't know why." He could see what the big ranchers were up to, but what was the end goal? And how the heck did Trampas play into things? "Are you *letting* Trampas steal our cattle?" Why couldn't he put the pieces in place? "You're protecting him...or tolerating him. I'm not sure which."

Huffing, Pa turned back to the bar and gripped it hard, turning his knuckles white. "You don't know what you're talking about."

"I know our yield is down fifteen percent from last year!" Thad shoved his hands into his pockets to hide his fists, took a breath, and forced himself to speak more softly. "Doesn't it bother you my counts never match Trampas's? Mine are always lower. The yield proves me right."

"Trampas is a good cowman. And *he* doesn't make mistakes." Thad fought the flinch that pulled at every muscle in his face. Pa snatched a bottle from the bar and stomped toward his room. He grabbed for the doorknob but paused. "A war is starting, Thad. I'll keep you and your brothers out of it...if I can."

Thad raked his fingers through his hair. Determined to get some answers, he rushed over and slammed the door shut in Pa's face. "If a war is the right thing, then why would you keep us out of it?"

Pa's lips tightened, narrowing to a sliver. He snatched the door open, forcing Thad to step aside. "I never said it was the right thing." He disappeared inside his room, slamming the door so hard glasses rattled on the bar.

Chapter Twenty

❦

Bull stormed into his home, as gratified as a conquering knight returning to his castle. Money was rolling in. An Italian gang trying to muscle in had been raided by the police. He'd found a new source for cheap whiskey.

All in a day's work.

Impressed with himself, he tossed his coat onto the hall table and yelled for attention.

"Hardy! Marie, where is my boy?"

Marie popped her head out of the den. "'E is in here, *monsieur*, in front of the fireplace. E is playing with the, um"—the maid scrambled for the right words—"logs. Lincoln Logs."

"Excellent." Bull shoved past the woman and strode to his son. "Good evening, Hardy."

"Hello, Daddy." The little boy looked up from his pile of logs that had not yet formed into any structure. "Will you play with me?"

"I have a moment, my lad." Bull stretched out on

the rug on the opposite side of the logs and pulled his pocket watch from his vest. Plenty of time. He did not need to meet at the docks till nine. A minute with his son, a nap, dinner, Charlene on his arm, and off they'd go to finalize some business. When he finally laid his head on his pillow sometime before dawn, he'd be another hundred thousand dollars richer.

Hardy shoved a pile of logs to Bull, who absently stacked them. As his son babbled away, Bull pondered the figures coming in from Fifteenth Street. He needed to change out the whores in the Chicago House. Their numbers were way down. The men were tired of them. New blood, that's what the House—

"I'm sorry, son. What did you say?" Surely, he hadn't heard right.

"The lady on the telephone said Mommy would be home soon. Do you know when?"

Bull snapped a log in his hand. His teeth felt like iron spikes in his mouth. "Marie!" he bellowed, rising to his feet. The maid rushed into the room, her face a mask of fear. Good. Bull grabbed her arm. "Did my wife call here? Did you speak with Mrs. Hendrick?"

Quaking, the woman shook her head. "I don't know. A woman called. She did not say 'er name."

"And you let her speak to my son?"

Behind them, Hardy burst into tears. Bull wanted to slap the kid across the room but took a deep breath and released Marie.

"I'm sorry. I did not know," the girl whined. "I thought it could be 'er. I did not know she should not speak to him."

"Shut the kid up." Livid, Bull marched across the

hall into his study and slammed the door. In two steps, he was at his desk. He snatched the telegram from Misery's sheriff out of his pocket.

G. Hendrick stopped here. Current whereabouts unknown. Sheriff, Misery, WY

Not only was the telegram something less-than-helpful, the sheriff had billed Bull for it. He crumpled it up and launched it into his fireplace. As the flames consumed the message, he wondered, *If Grace wasn't in Misery, where had she gone? She didn't have enough money to start back to Chicago, did she?*

He realized his mistake in not giving the sheriff any notice of Grace's arrival. Worse, he hadn't asked the lawman to keep tabs on her. He hadn't thought it would be necessary. In a town of a hundred people, Grace couldn't simply disappear.

However, that was irrelevant. Bottom line, Bull didn't know where Grace was.

And that would not do.

❦

The group of ranch hands headed back to the Lazy H after the gala in Sheridan was a sorry lot. Grace followed from the rear, listening to the cowboys commiserate about the saloon they'd invaded after the *respectable* party was over. While Thad and Adam had retired, Nick and the boys had painted the town.

She could have laughed, watching them ride, alternately holding their heads and their stomachs, moaning, groaning, and complaining about their poor choices. It was proving to be a long journey...for them all.

Adam, blessed with youth and energy, spent the first ten miles peppering Grace with questions about Susanna. Where did they go? What did they do? Was she nice? More lies tumbled out of Grace's mouth.

Thad had barely said two words to her when they'd saddled up back in Sheridan. Now, with the road to the Diamond R coming up, it didn't appear he would add anything to the minor greetings from this morning. She supposed he was embarrassed, figuring that Grace would have told Greg everything.

She hung her head and sighed. What a mess, but it was better this way. Grace would concentrate on earning her pay from Raney. She should have some money waiting when she got back to the ranch and then, in another month, another payment. That would be enough to get her back to Chicago.

Thad veered off from the group, looped around, and trotted up beside Grace, a troubled groove in his brow.

"Did your sister tell you anything about last night?"

Grace shrugged. "Only that she did a little dancing."

Thad chewed on that for a moment. "That all?"

"Yep."

"This fella back in Chicago. Any chance she'll go back to him?"

Grace tapped her fingers on the saddle horn and realized, finally, she could tell the pure, unadulterated truth about something. "She wants to get her...belongings, but, after that, no matter what it takes," Grace cut her eyes at Thad, "she's gonna slip away or die tryin'."

"Slip away? If she's done with him, why not just divorce him?"

Like she hadn't run the scenario through her mind a thousand times. The mere use of the word had gotten Grace her worst beating to date. Bull was always careful not to strike her in the face, but anything below the neck was fair game, and he knew how to play the game. Broken ribs, dislocated shoulders...

Grace flinched and backed away from the memories. "If I—*she*—she ever served Bull with papers, not only would he not sign them, he would come after her." Talk of Bull made the vast, empty hills suddenly eerie. She felt vulnerable...and exposed. "Bull doesn't believe in losing."

"She can't hide from him the rest of her life. That's no life at all."

Irritation flared in Grace. Thad Walker and his opinions. What did he know anyway? "I'll be sure to share your keen insight with my sister."

Done with the conversation, Grace moved to kick her horse, but Adam trotted up, grinning like the Cheshire Cat.

"Hey, Thad, an hour one way or the other won't make any difference. Let's hit the pools."

Grace's stomach dropped to her stirrups. She knew exactly what pools Adam meant. Raney had pointed them out the other day...the hot springs on the edge of her property. Grace had longed to visit them but was afraid of being caught in a compromising situation.

"I don't know, Adam..." Thad swished his reins back and forth. "Pa's expecting us by suppertime." But Grace heard the resolve in his voice softening to the temptation of warm, bubbly water. "We don't have to stay long, I guess."

Adam whooped and hollered to the other men, "Let's go, boys!"

The men kicked their horses into gallops and followed after Adam. They left the road and high-tailed it across an open, rolling hill.

Chuckling, Thad looked at Grace. He opened his mouth to speak but bit it off. "You're as white as a weddin' gown."

"I told you I don't like to swim." Panic laced her voice. *Calm down*, she scolded. *Calm down.*

He sucked on his cheek and eyed her suspiciously. "That's not gonna wash this time. Granted, you might not be fond of water, but these pools are the size of big bathtubs and about as deep. So what are you really afraid of?"

His eyes were more of gunmetal-blue now, and they carried a warning: no more lies. But she couldn't tell him the truth. "I..."

He leaned forward attentively.

"I..." She licked her lips. "I..." The idea struck her like a lightning bolt and the lie gushed out. "I have a scar. A terrible scar."

His brow arched with surprise. "That's not such a—"

"I'm embarrassed by it. And I don't want you and the others to rib me over it."

Thad lifted his hat and set it back down, as if the

action helped him think. "I would say you're among friends, but they *can* be a might childish. Trampas, just plain mean." He thought a moment longer then turned his horse to follow the others. "Come on."

Grace recoiled. "I'm not going."

He pulled the reins up, spun his horse around to her. An impish grin flirted with his lips and that wonderful dimple appeared. "You trust me, kid?"

She searched his face, debating, but, in truth, Grace knew the answer. "Yeah."

He beamed with satisfaction. "Then come on."

He kicked his horse to a gallop and Grace followed.

In mere minutes, they crested a hill and she saw the cowboys' horses tied to trees and men flinging off their clothes.

"I can't do this," she whispered breathlessly, but Thad charged right in among them. Compelled, because she didn't know how to get out of this, Grace trailed behind.

Down in the hollow where the pools were located, thick steam rose from each circle of water. Thad dismounted and winked at Grace. "Take off your boots and your coat."

Puzzled but willing to go on a little faith, she climbed down and removed the items, draping her coat over her saddle horn.

"Socks, too." He pointed at her feet.

She noticed the men watching her and was horrified to realize they were in various stages of undress. She quickly bent over to hide her shock and saw Adam's bare legs on the other side of her horse.

Naked? They're all going naked as jaybirds?

She knew her eyes had to be the size of half-dollars. Panic choked her reason. Thad reached over and snatched the sock off her raised foot. Cold air chilled her toes. Without any warning, he tossed her over his shoulder, snatched off her other sock, and started walking.

"Put me down, Thad Walker!" Grace kicked and yelled, trying her best not to squeal like a girl. The hands exploded with laughter. Naked, they pointed and guffawed. She was horrified. She squeezed her eyes shut, mortified. Did these men—or just men in general—have no shame?

Thad tossed Grace, and she landed with a splash in shocking, breath-stealing *hot* water. She sputtered and splashed and found her feet and stood. The water came to her chest...and felt absolutely glorious.

She sought out Thad, but the steam from the pool was so thick she could barely make out his shadow nearby.

"Welcome to Wyoming, Greg," he yelled, sounding positively exuberant.

More raucous laughter. Shadows appeared behind Thad, moving, sailing through the air. She scrubbed her face with water to avoid seeing the bodies that flew at her. The sound of splashes and whooping and hollering circulated all around her. The water in her pool sloshed violently. Good grief, they were in here with her!

"Just a little initiation."

Grace opened one eye and peeked in the direction of Thad's voice. He had squatted down on the edge of the pool. The steam moved and undulated around him, obscuring him intermittently.

"Give me your clothes and I'll lay 'em out on the trees."

Grace boiled with fury. "You think that was funny? Trust me, you said. I'll freeze to death between here and Raney's. Again."

"I sort of thought you'd be used to a dunkin' by now."

She certainly preferred the hot water to the cold, but that was beside the point. She moved closer to him and whispered through clenched teeth, "How am I supposed to get *out* of the pool."

"I got you in. I'll get you out."

He grinned, the dimple appeared again, and, somehow, Grace couldn't hold on to her anger.

But she absolutely was going to hang on to her long johns. After a few attempts to talk her out of them, Thad gave up. He disappeared with her wet clothes into the fog.

"Don't take it too hard," Adam said from somewhere behind her, and she spun. "It happens to us all. Just a joke." Adam swam closer, appearing out of the fog like an apparition. "You should've given him your long johns."

The boy was bare above the water, shoulders and most of his chest slick with moisture, and she assumed he was bare below. Beside herself over this mess, Grace averted her eyes, following the swirls in the mist. This whole situation made her want to slither under a rock.

"It's pretty nice to climb into dry underwear," he

continued. "It won't chafe so bad if the rest of your things aren't dry."

Grace nodded stiffly and moved away from him, hugging the bank. Through the steam, she saw a foot appear, test the water, then sink down, a bare leg slowly following. Afraid of what else she might see, she spun in the opposite direction.

"Sweeney," Thad hollered, sinking into the water, "You're usually out first. Be sure to build a fire."

"Yes, sir," a disembodied voice answered. "You can count on it."

Thad sighed, a content sound that made Grace envious, and leaned back, his bare arms spread on the bank. After a moment, he ran a dripping hand through his gold locks and winked at her. "Well, Buttercup, what do you think now?"

Grace hunkered down a little lower in the water and didn't answer. Instead, she listened quietly to Thad and Adam talking ranch business. Without any warning, Nick appeared out of the mist and climbed down into the water with them, barely giving Grace time to avert her eyes. He glistened, and his dark hair dripped with water. Apparently, he'd been relaxing in a different pool but moved when the talk circled around to cattle.

Grace splashed her face for a distraction, wishing she could block all that she had seen in the last half hour. More than *any* woman should *ever* see in a lifetime. If so much hadn't been riding on this ruse, the absurdity of her predicament would have been laughable.

"Well, I think we'd better get started home."

173

Thad's observation brought Grace back to the conversation.

Nick took a quick dip beneath the steaming water. Adam splashed his face and nodded. "All right, big brother."

The young boy crossed the pool and climbed out. Grace stared intently into the water and steam as, one by one, the cowboys hauled out of the warm, caressing waters and retrieved their clothes from bushes and saddle horns.

"You comin', Thad?" Adam asked, holding his clothes in a bunch at his waist.

Thad waved lazily at Grace. "I thought I'd make sure Buttercup got on his way without any hypothermia."

Adam nodded, gave Grace a quick adios salute, and then disappeared into the mist. As the noise and activity faded, she finally started to relax. But her face was flushed and the water was beginning to drive her body temperature up. She couldn't stay much longer, either.

The steam shifted and she caught Thad staring at her.

"You can leave any time, Buttercup. They're all gone."

He'd gotten her in.

He was getting her out.

"Yes. Yeah, I'll go...one more minute."

Though it was hot, the water was relaxing, and this was the warmest she'd been since arriving in Wyoming.

A few minutes of companionable silence slipped by

before he said, "Mind if I ask about this terrible, ugly scar you've got?"

Grace wanted to sink below the water. She should've known he'd ask at some point. She didn't have to go far, though, to come up with a story. It just wasn't *her* story. "A log rolled out of the fireplace when I was two. Burned my side pretty badly."

Thad sucked in a breath. "Ouch. Burns are the worst. Take forever to heal."

"It took months," she said softly, remembering the agony a neighbor's daughter had suffered one winter in Pennsylvania.

As if sensing she truly did need her privacy, Thad pushed off the side of the pool. "Well, this is always the hardest part. Getting out and putting on cold clothes, or in your case, *very* cold clothes."

Grace spoke just as the white of his waistline broke the surface, and he halted. "Thanks, Thad. I appreciate what you did." She took an instant to appreciate the chiseled muscles of his back and the white line at his waist but then spun away before she saw more, surprised at herself for even thinking about peeking.

He splashed her playfully as he climbed out. "Your secret is safe with me, little man."

Chapter Twenty-One

❦

"Well, how was the party?" Raney paused in mopping the kitchen floor and straightened. "Did you see your sister?"

Grace shuffled to the table and sat down. The feeling that everything had spiraled out of control with Thad both crushed her spirits and filled her with wonder. She hated lying to him, loved being with him. She couldn't feel like this. Not now. Not, well...ever.

She met Raney's puzzled, expectant gaze. "Oh, I'm sorry. Yes, ma'am. I had a grand time. It was..." What had Adam called it? "...a real hoedown. Thank you for letting me use your room."

Raney shrugged and commenced mopping again. "Well, my hip was bothering me too bad. Didn't want it to go to waste. My dues to the WSGA paid for it. 'Sides, you don't need to be bunkin' with those rough-talking cowboys. Speaking of which, your sister...?"

"My sister. Yes, she's fine," Grace finished the

woman's thought for her. "She's working at Dolly's Café."

"Dolly's Café?" Raney dropped the mop in a bucket and stepped over to the stove. She dried her hands on her apron, slapped a piece of cold ham onto a biscuit, and handed it to Grace. "That place burned down last month."

"Oh, well, I—I must have the name wrong then. Some café."

"Only other place to eat in Sheridan—" Raney stopped mid-sentence.

Grace steeled herself against the challenge she could see on the woman's face. Instead, surprisingly, Raney abruptly changed the subject. "Otis is about to throw a shoe and we need to clean Dandy's hooves. You up for it?" Raney cocked her head to one side, a hopeful, cautious lift to one brow. "You have cleaned a horse's hooves before?"

"Yes, ma'am."

"Well, that's somethin'."

Finally, a task on Raney's ranch that Grace had experience with. She pulled Dandy's back hoof up between her knees and commenced scraping out the muck. A few feet away, Raney worked on removing Otis's damaged shoe, one stubborn nail at a time.

"So...Greg...I have surely appreciated your help around here."

Grace didn't slow down in her work, but she heard

the regret lacing Raney's voice. Bracing herself for the worst, she scraped a little harder.

"And you're showin' yourself to be a right fine hand," the woman continued. "Oh, you're a little rough around the edges yet, but you work hard and you don't complain. Eventually, you're going to be a right-skilled cowboy."

Grace dropped the hoof and stood up. "Raney, are you firing me?"

Raney muttered a curse under her breath and released her pony's hoof, standing up with the old shoe in her hand. She tossed it into a pile of iron and dropped the nail-puller into her apron.

"No...but you may wanna quit after you hear this." She huffed a breath. "I need to cut your wages.

"Cut?"

Raney wiped her hands on her pants and ambled over to Grace, resting her elbows on Dandy's rump. Ranch life and all its worries showed on her face, in the gray hair at her temples and the lines running deeper around her features. "I haven't wanted to 'fess up, but I've had trouble making my mortgage payments, and I haven't wanted to sell any more land. Martin Riley, down at the bank, he was carrying the note, giving me time to sell the herd in the spring." Raney chewed on her bottom lip and patted Dandy's back nervously. "Martin died last week. The bank's replaced him with a fella from Denver. He's calling my note."

Grace and Raney didn't talk much the rest of the afternoon. The woman had told her to take a week to think things over. Dinner was quiet as well, as both of them dealt with their burdens. Though Grace sensed there was something else, another shoe to drop.

Raney shooed Grace out of the kitchen so she could clean up. Feeling as lost as an orphan, Grace wandered out to the front porch and tried to lose herself in the night sky. She hoped the aurora borealis would reappear and assure her that not everything had collapsed into hopelessness and chaos.

There were no wavering, shimmering lights, but the stars twinkled and glimmered as they had for thousands of years. She found some peace in that.

Raney wandered out after a few minutes and drew up beside her, a cigarette smoking in her left hand. "This mess sure is a helluva note."

"My hu—uhm, brother-in-law, Bull, is always saying, 'play the hand you're dealt.'" That seemed a trite and pointless comment now. As if they had a choice.

"Yep," Raney nodded, "I guess the trick is figuring out which cards to keep and which ones to toss." She took a drag from the cigarette and slowly released the smoke.

"What about the Walkers? I know they think the world of you, Raney. Could you borrow the money till the spring?"

"Thought about selling Earl the whole herd, but..."

Grace inhaled a deep, bracing breath, knowing this was the other shoe. "But...?"

Raney took another puff, a clear delay tactic.

"We're missing twenty, twenty-five head. Maybe more. I don't have enough cattle to sell to cover the note."

Grace's mouth fell open. "What do you mean they're missing?"

Raney tossed the cigarette to the ground like she was batting away a wasp and crushed it beneath her toes. "Rustlers."

Chapter Twenty-Two

❦

Pa did not join his sons for breakfast, a rare occurrence. Wondering if he was a glutton for punishment, Thad tossed his napkin to the table and told Nick and Adam to meet him out by the barn in half an hour.

Walking softly, he approached his father's office. Muffled voices, angry voices, stopped his hand as he was about to knock.

"I told you, Trampas, never her. I've got that handled."

"You want her spread, don't you? I can make it look like an accident. Just like Bill and Mag—"

A smack and a grunt, followed by a crash, brought Thad bursting into the room. He skidded to a stop. Pa stood over Trampas, who lay on the floor among the shattered remains of a coffee table, blood trickling from his mouth.

"What's going on here, Pa?"

His father flexed a bloody right hand. "Trampas is

taking me to the train station. Ain't that right, Trampas?"

The man rubbed his jaw and climbed to his feet. "Yes, sir."

❦

Thad leaned his forehead on the barn, his hat sliding off into the dust. Rage and despair boiled in him.

He knew what he'd heard.

Trampas had killed Maggie to get Bill to sell.

So who was the *her* Pa had mentioned?

Never her.

Raney?

Was Trampas an over-eager hired gun? Was one of the other cattle barons paying him to knock down independents...or was Pa?

Trampas had not bad-mouthed Bothwell one time, even after Ella's lynching. Merely said he couldn't stomach it, but even then, he hadn't had much outrage in his voice. Maybe he'd had a hand in her murder after all. Maybe murder was what he did.

God, help me sort out this tangled web. And please don't let any of it lead back to Pa.

"Oh, gee, Thad?" Adam slipped his arms around his big brother and tried to pull him upright. "You okay? Is it somethin' you ate?"

"Get off me." He pushed the boy away like he was untangling from a snake. "I'm all right, I'm all right," he protested as Adam fought to hang on. Huffing and shooting his little brother the stink eye, Thad leaned over and snatched his hat from the dirt. "I was just thinkin'." He crammed the Stetson onto his head and brushed past his little brother. "Tell Nick I rode over to Raney's. I'll be back by supper."

☙❧

"Raney, we need to talk." Thad removed his hat and held it to his chest. "It's important."

An axe rested on the woman's shoulder as she balanced a piece of wood on the chopping block. Heeding Thad, she dropped it into the stump and wiped her hands. "I can do this later. Come on in the house and I'll make us some coffee."

☙❧

Thad supposed he shouldn't have been surprised when Raney didn't bat an eye at his concerns. But he was. Nick, and now Raney, had seen something in Pa that had unsettled them. Thad had wanted to blame his own unease on Trampas, that *he* was the troublemaker.

Raney merely shrugged at the suggestion as she shuffled around the kitchen. "Your pa's never let anybody lead him into anything." She set two cups of coffee on the table, sat down across from Thad, and stirred sugar into her steaming mug. "The SGA is planning something. We all know it."

The crow's feet around Raney's eyes had deepened some, Thad thought, and a pained frown creased her brow. But more noticeably, she wasn't sitting as straight as normal, as if something weighed her down.

"Things are gettin' worse, son. The cattle barons

are pushing and pushing. I thought maybe they'd let sleeping dogs lie after Ella and Jake's deaths." She drummed her fingers on the table in a restless rhythm. "Then they took poor Tom Waggoner in June. His wife said none of his stock was missing." She leaned toward Thad, her voice rising with anger. "What kind of rustlers hang a man and leave his stock alone? It's Wolcott and Hesse...they're growin' bold again. Especially since they've seen your pa pick up three ranches in the last two years."

"He got those ranches fair and square, Raney."

She sagged and looked at him like he was a daft child. "You mean he paid fair money for 'em. But you need to dig deeper. What prompted those ranchers to sell? Couple that with what you heard Trampas say... and *I'm* missing cattle now." She let that sink in, then rose and walked over to the kitchen sink. She gazed out at the horses in the back pasture and shook her head. "I used to think the sun rose and set on your pa, but I toyed with his heart, as a young girl is wont to do. I shouldn't have been surprised when he married Lucille. I loved her like a sister, but it hurt." She exhaled a long breath, as if trying to expel the pain. "Jake got me over Earl. He was a good man."

Raney rounded on Thad, grief and disappointment etched on her face. "I believe your pa has lost his soul, Thad. Don't make it easier for him by lying to yourself."

Thad ran his fingers around the rim of his mug. He knew, deep down, in a place he never wanted to search, that Raney was right about Pa. He didn't know how in the world he was going to be able to talk to

him about any of this, much less get him to...*to what?*
Stand down? Turn Trampas in? Turn against the SGA? At
least Raney was aware something was afoot. She'd stay
alert, warn the others if need be. And she wasn't
alone now.

Or was she?

"Where's that hired hand of yours?"

She worked her jaw back and forth for a moment.
"Sent him into town for some supplies."

Her steady gaze softened, tweaking Thad's
curiosity.

"What?"

"You met his sister at the dance. Did she tell you
where she's working?"

"Dolly's Café."

Raney sighed and ran a hand over her mouth, then
folded her arms on the table. "Dolly's burned down a
week before the dance."

Thad's face went slack. "What? Then she
must be..."

"Waiting on tables in some other fine establishment in Sheridan?"

"Ah, you know there ain't—" An icicle stabbed him
in the heart. He thought about the options for a gal in
Sheridan...and was amazed that hope bobbed to the
surface again. It seemed he couldn't believe the worst
of Grace Hendrick, either. "The Golden Lady does
have a restaurant, Raney. I don't think all the waitress-
es..." He let the silence finish the thought.

Raney absently turned her coffee cup around and
around on the table. "I just hate that Greg felt like he
couldn't tell me. You, I can understand, the way you've

been carrying on about the girl. He didn't want to break your heart."

Thad pushed his coffee away but stared a hole through it. Was Grace who she said she was, or was she a liar, too, like Pa? Thad felt the foundation of the things he believed in dissolving like salt beneath his feet.

❦

Grace read the sign hanging on the café door. Then read it again.

Waitress wanted.

There it was.

A choice.

A chance.

She could walk away from Raney and the woman's burdens. She could leave her to sell her ranch or fight the bank for it till she lost it. It shouldn't matter to her that Raney wanted nothing more in the world than to hang on to the Diamond R.

Grace needed to think about Hardy. If Raney couldn't pay her, then, for Pete's sake, surely taking a job with real wages was the smart thing to do.

How had a simple trip into Misery turned into such a pivotal moment?

She took a halting step toward the door but had to quickly move aside for some cowboys exiting the restaurant. Her back against the wall, she wondered why this was so hard. Just go in there, smile, show the owner how she could commit six orders to memory and easily carry four plates at once.

Grace shook her head and pondered her dusty boots. Even if she could get the owner to see past the short hair and dirty clothes, this was not where Grace wanted to be.

She exhaled, letting the opportunity go, and pushed off the wall.

She would stick with Raney, at least for another month or two.

"'Scuse me, young fella."

Grace flinched. She knew the sheriff's voice and had avoided him like the plague on her visits to Misery, lest he peer too closely and wonder if they'd met.

"Boy?" the lawman said, irritable now.

Grace faced the sheriff's scrutiny. "Yes, sir?"

His buttons still on the verge of popping off his grimy shirt, Sheriff Phillips studied her top to bottom and back again. Frowning, he shook his head as if she didn't add up. "Folks told me you came into town with a sister. I need to know where she's at."

"Why?"

The sheriff's hand struck like a snake, the slap stinging Grace's cheek and making her ears ring. "Don't sass me, boy. I'm the sheriff. I can ask anything I want to, of anybody. Now, one more time"—he leaned in—"the *last* time. Did you come into town with a sister?"

Grace knew it would do no good to lie. In fact, it would only complicate her life even more. Rubbing her burning cheek, she nodded. "Yes, sir."

"Where is she?"

"I've got a right to know why you're asking after my sister."

The sheriff chuckled and tapped his breast pocket. "Her husband wired me some money to determine her whereabouts. Now, a man's got a right to know that about his wife."

"If I tell you, will you leave her alone?"

"I don't want nothing from her. Her husband just wants to know where she's working."

Grace's mind raced. The sheriff didn't seem interested in doing any extra work. Perhaps if she sold him a bill of goods, he would be satisfied with that and not track her down. "She's waiting tables over in Sheridan. At Dolly's Café." Grace realized immediately that was not the answer Bull wanted. Maybe it was time to play his game. "No, that's not exactly true." The sheriff's brow lifted, and Grace sighed dramatically. "She's gone wrong, Sheriff. She's working in a...in a..." Grace shook her head as if she couldn't bring herself to say it.

The sheriff nodded. "I see." He scratched his scruffy jaw and pondered the development. "Reckon how he'll take the news?"

"I imagine, Sheriff, that is exactly the news he wants."

His expression lightened considerably. "Do you happen to recall the name of the establishment?"

Grace feigned ignorance with a shrug.

"Maybe the Bird Cage?" the sheriff prodded. "Or the Golden Lady?"

"Golden Lady." Grace snapped her fingers. "That sounds right."

Is this sheriff an idiot?

Bull had to fight to keep from ripping the telegram in his hand into a thousand pieces. He waved it at Lonnie. "Did you read this?"

"No." Bull raised a doubtful eyebrow. Lonnie shrugged. "Well, I did catch the brother part."

Bewildered, Bull walked around his desk and sat down. He read the telegram aloud, more for his benefit than Lonnie's. "*The brother informs me Mrs. Hendrick working at Golden Lady...not a respectable establishment.*" Bull picked up the .32 sitting on his desk and twirled it around his index finger.

Brother? Whose brother? The sheriff's? Grace's? But Grace had no brother. These telegrams were clear as mud, and when things weren't clear, Bull got suspicious. He growled at the inconvenience ahead and stood. "Pack your bag, Lonnie boy, we're going to the land of cowboys and cattle."

The last thing in the world Thad wanted to do was shatter his brothers' respect for their father, but he didn't want to carry this burden alone, either. Over dinner, he told them everything he knew, everything Pa had said, everything he'd overheard.

What if he was wrong? What if he'd misunderstood or misinterpreted?

No. Coupled with Raney's comments, the details were coming together in Thad's head, and the picture they were painting turned his stomach. He stabbed a steak and slapped it on his plate with a whole lot more anger than hunger.

Nick and Adam's dour expressions echoed his thoughts. Nick, especially, seemed troubled. He dropped his fork onto his plate with a loud clatter. "Pa's lost his way, Thad. I've known it for a while now. It's not just about holding on to the ranch. He wants more range. A lot more."

Adam twirled his fork in his beans, nodding. "It's like an obsession," he whispered. "I think he thinks he'll live forever as long as the ranch goes on."

"Reasons don't matter." Nick splayed his hands on the dinner table. "I was there when they cut Waggoner down from that tree and brought him home to his wife. The rope dang near severed his head." He pursed his lips as if physically holding back his rage. "And I'm the one who found Maggie. If the SGA is sanctioning any of that...if Pa's going along with it—"

"We'll confront him with what we know. Get him to do the right thing." The voice of reason, Thad believed the battle for Pa's soul wasn't lost just yet. Nick and Adam's blank stares said they didn't necessarily agree. "*I* haven't given up on him. Not yet. When he gets back from Cheyenne, we'll talk to him. Make him listen."

Slowly, Nick stood up, squeezing his dinner napkin in his hand. "I don't see Pa going against the SGA, Thad, but you better pray he does. Otherwise, he's liable to tear this family apart." He tossed the napkin onto his plate and stormed from the room.

Chapter Twenty-Three

❧

Twilight settled on Raney's as Grace rolled in with the empty hay wagon. The herd was in the south section, munching contentedly on stacks of timothy. Here, in the barnyard, the chickens were scurrying back to the roost, and Dog had clambered up the front steps to take his place for the night. A welcoming quiet, framed by the jingle of horse harnesses and squeaky wheels, made Grace feel at home.

If only...

"You get the stock fed?" Raney called from the chicken coop.

Grace raised her hat. "Yes, ma'am."

"All right. Put the horses up and wash your hands. Supper's eggs and bacon tonight. Keepin' it simple."

"That's fine with me." Grace parked the wagon outside the barn so she could easily re-hitch the horses in the morning and move some barbed wire out to the

Crazy Woman section. "Come on, Dandy. Let's get you settled for the night."

She unbuckled, unhitched, and untied until she had Dandy free of the harness. Dog-tired from pitching hay all day, Grace clutched the mare's halter and tugged. Dandy resisted and shook her head a few times, as if she didn't really want to go.

"Dandy," Grace tightened her grip on the halter and pulled harder, "Come on now. We don't have time for this."

The horse complied grudgingly and trudged beside Grace into the barn, now awash in shadows. Three steps into the darkness, though, Dandy bowed up again and grumbled a deep, throaty warning. The horse pinned her ears back.

An instant later, horrific screeching and braying erupted from the feed room as a dark mass bolted through the door. Dandy jerked away from Grace, spun, and backed up to the wall, pinning Grace and squeezing the breath from her.

The horse squealed a terrified, high-pitched scream, and reared. Grace saw the flash of hooves as the horse and a randy mule clashed. Before she could dive clear of the fight, she caught a hoof to her chest. The pain buckled her knees, smothering her scream as the air whooshed out of her lungs. She gasped, or tried to, but her lungs wouldn't function. Sliding to the ground, she clutched at the hay and tried to crawl to safety, but her body moved as if it was stuck in molasses. Panic and confusion overrode rational thought.

*Air...*she screamed in her head, *I...need...air. My lungs...*

"Hey! Hey! Hey!" Raney yelled. Grace heard the crack of a whip, once, twice, and thought the scuffling animals shifted away, but she couldn't be sure. Desperate for a breath, she felt as if Dandy was sitting on her chest. She couldn't breathe, she couldn't see. She reached for Raney but found darkness instead.

☙❧

Grace sucked in a deep breath of glorious, fresh, invigorating air...and sat bolt-upright in bed. Her mind reeled with confusion.

Panting, she clutched the blanket and looked down. Her shirt hung open, exposing much too much cleavage. Gathering the garment, she sucked in another deep, satisfying breath and tried to think.

Then the pain pounded its way to the front of her mind like a crazed marching band. Her ribs ached ferociously and she groaned, but at least she could breathe.

She touched her side and tried to focus. She had no memory of how she'd made it here from the barn.

"How ya feel?"

Raney's voice nearly made Grace jump out of her skin. She clutched her shirt tighter and discovered her boss staring at her from the doorway.

"Fine." Grace swallowed and calmed herself. "Better, anyway. I can breathe, but my ribs hurt something awful."

"Yeah, you've got some good bruising around your

chest." Raney ambled into the small room and took a seat in the rocking chair at the foot of the bed. "You'll be all right, just sore for a day or two."

Grace heard the stiffness in Raney's voice and dropped her head in shame. The binding she wrapped herself in had been removed. There was no way Raney didn't know the truth.

The woman leaned back in the rocker and it squeaked beneath her weight. She sighed, a heavy sound full of disappointment. Grace kept her head down. On top of everything else, Raney had to deal with this now.

"So, I might be a smidgen slow, but I ain't stupid." The woman paused, waiting perhaps for Grace to look up, but she couldn't. Not yet. "I reckon your name ain't Greg. Grace, I expect?"

Everything in Grace broke, and her house of lies crumbled. Tears filled her eyes and a sob escaped her. Ashamed and humiliated, she hid her face in her hands and wept like a little girl.

"Oh, Raney, I'm so sorry." Misery strangled her voice. "I never meant...all I wanted...please forgive..."

Her throat squeezed tight and she couldn't finish. For the first time in months, Grace gave up the battle to be strong and let it all out in a soul-shaking, crying jag.

"Oh, child," Raney blurted, rushing to hug Grace. "There, there." She wrapped Grace in a tight embrace and rocked with her. "Shhhh, there now." She rubbed Grace's back lightly. "I know this has something to do with that husband of yours. You must be pretty desperate to try to pull off a charade like this."

"He has my son," Grace blubbered into Raney's shoulder. "I just want to get him back."

"By working on a ranch as a man?" Raney sounded utterly thunderstruck.

Grace shook her head and pulled away, sniffling, fighting to gather her wits. "He thinks I'm a prostitute."

❦

Raney made coffee for her and Grace and brought the steaming cups into the bedroom. Handing one to Grace, she sat down once more in the rocking chair. "Let's try this again, shall we? Why don't you start at the beginning and make some sense this time?"

Grace slowed her heart and took a sip of the warm, comforting coffee. A bite at the end revealed a little something extra in the cup. "Bull thought I was having an affair with my photographer—"

"Were you?"

"No. I would have been within my rights to. There's never been any fidelity from Bull...but no. Of course, the truth didn't matter to him. He sent me here and said if I tried to come back and take Hardy, he'd ship him off to a boarding school and I'd never see him again."

Raney took a sip and scratched her head. "How does he know you're even here? How did he know you'd come all this way?"

"I was instructed to check in with the sheriff, which I did. Bull, however, has since checked on me to make sure I was right where he wanted me. Which is why I told the sheriff I—Grace—was working over at the Golden Lady. If Bull thinks I'm miserable, maybe he'll leave me alone."

Raney scrunched her face up in disapproval. "I don't see how..." she shook her head and started again. "What was your plan, besides to work for me?"

"I wanted to save enough money to sneak back to Chicago and run away with Hardy."

Raney blew on her coffee and shook her head. "And here I am cuttin' your wages. If this situation, yours and mine, don't beat all." She set her mug on a small barrel doubling as a table, slapped the rocking chair's arm, and stood. "Reckon I know what I've got to do."

"What?"

Raney marched up to Grace and squeezed her arm. "I'm gonna see Earl. I'll get a loan and some cattle from him. We'll make this place pay, and we'll get your boy."

"Aw, Raney, I can't let you do that—"

She cut Grace's protest with another squeeze. "Hush. I didn't realize till just now how much of the fight has gone outta me." She shook her head. "I'm old, but I ain't dead. Let's give these rustlers and these cattle barons and, yes, even your husband, a reason to fear the women of the Diamond R."

Chapter Twenty-Four

❧

Bull and Lonnie marched across the porch of the neatly painted Victorian house they'd been assured was the home of the Golden Lady and let themselves in. As they removed their hats, a beautiful middle-aged woman wearing a mere hint of makeup and a tasteful, high-necked dress met them in the foyer. In spite of all the horses tied out front, Bull wondered if they were in the right place.

"Gentlemen, how may I be of service?"

Bull eyed the place. To his right, diners—all male—clinked silverware and laughed over their meals. To his left, he saw a young lady draped seductively over a settee in an ornately decorated parlor. Slowly, she pulled a curl over her shoulder and gave Bull a sultry wink.

Oh, yeah, right place.

"I'm looking for someone, a young lady by the name of Grace Hendrick."

The woman's face hardened a bit. "I'm sorry, we don't have anyone here by that name."

Bull supposed Grace might have used a false one. "Real pretty gal. Strawberry hair, big, green eyes, would have showed up sometime in the last month."

"I'm sorry. I haven't hired anyone new since September."

Twirling his hat in his hand, Bull wondered about his next step. "Well, long as we're here, we'll grab lunch." His attention drifted back to the girl in the parlor. "And, maybe, we'll indulge in your entertainment."

The woman brightened. "Lovely. Follow me, and I'll seat you."

While Bull waited on his steak and Lonnie his fried chicken, both men sat in silence. The more Bull thought about things, the angrier he got. Tapping his fingers on the shot glass full of whiskey, he tried to piece things together. Somehow, Grace was attempting to throw him off her trail. Maybe the sheriff was a liar, or simply an incompetent boob, but Bull didn't think so.

"What do you think, boss?" Lonnie asked softly.

Bull raised the whiskey to his lips and tossed it back. The burn cleared his head a bit. "I believe we need to see the sheriff over in Misery, after all." He flipped the shot glass upside down and clinked it on the table. "Let's find out what he and my missus are up to."

"You think 'e's hiding Mrs. 'endrick?"

Bull ran a beefy hand through his black curls,

pulling them off his forehead. "If he is, I don't think he'll need to worry about running for re-election."

⚜

Thad inhaled deeply, but the uneasy jitters in his gut didn't leave. He had to be some kind of glutton for punishment. Still determined, he grabbed the door knob of the Golden Lady. He didn't care if anyone saw him. All he wanted was the truth about Grace. It seemed important, as if knowing what was going on with her would help him settle things with Pa when he returned from Cheyenne. Or maybe he was so afraid of what was happening to the Walkers that he needed to have one person to believe in.

Please, Jesus, don't let her be here.

"Well, bend me over and slap my cheeks." Madge drifted out of the parlor on Thad's left, an expression of complete disbelief on her stoic, regal face. "A Walker has darkened my door. Is it your birthday, Thad?"

Thad snatched the hat off his head, unsure if that was necessary in the presence of a woman like Madge, but he was still a gentleman. "No, ma'am, it's nothing like that. I'm looking for someone."

Madge rested a hand on her hip and ambled over to Thad, taking him in, inch by inch, up one side and down the other. "What a shame you boys never come see me. I'd wait on you personally."

Thad pursed his lips, biting back the urge to tell the woman he was in a hurry. He'd heard she was a sucker for compliments and figured maybe the right remark could grease the rails. "If I was of a mind, ma'am, you certainly would be my first choice."

The woman seemed to float an inch off the ground, and her whole face softened. The hand moved from her hip to her bosom. "Oh, my, and a sweet-talker, too." She gave him a sultry wink but then sighed softly. "So, any chance you're here about a pretty gal, strawberry hair, big, green eyes? Would've shown up in the last month?"

Thad's mouth fell open in shock, but then the reason for Madge's apt description sunk his spirits. "I guess that means she's here."

Madge smiled slyly. "No, it means you're the second person to come asking today, and I'll tell you like I told him. I haven't hired anybody new since September."

Thad crushed his hat in his hands. "Somebody else is looking for her?" He couldn't pull the connection together. Who would come for her other than—

"You could compare notes," Madge suggested, motioning toward the dining room. "He and his friend are having lunch."

Thad hurried over to a large fern and peered through the leaves. Madge came up beside him and pointed. "The big man, dark hair, by the window."

Bull Hendrick. It had to be.

Thad could see where the man got his nickname. He had shoulders that would intimidate a grizzly. With thick, black hair and eyebrows, and a scowl that was as much a part of his face as his nose, he truly did remind Thad of a Brahma bull. An angry one.

He pulled back and dragged his hand over his

mouth. Bull was here hunting for Grace. But if Grace wasn't here, then where the heck was she?

Greg would know. And they had to get to Grace to warn her.

"I heard them say they were going to see the sheriff over in Misery."

"The sheriff?" A memory smacked Thad. The way Greg had hid his face from the sheriff in Cheyenne, like he was trying to avoid being spotted, maybe by any lawman. He dropped his hat back on his head. "Much obliged, Madge."

"Anytime, young Walker. *Any*time." Something about Madge reminded Thad of a cougar watching a rabbit and he backed out of the Golden Lady.

Chapter Twenty-Five

✦

A string of horses, a half-dozen or so, tied in front of the Number Nine, drew Thad to a stop. An uneasy feeling wiggling in his stomach, he nudged Bo forward and casually surveyed the brands on the animals. The Circle T, the 2U, the HK, and the Lazy H. All big outfits. At least two of the horses belonged to ranch foremen, specifically Mike Shonsey and Trampas, two men not very fond of each other.

The door to the Number Nine burst open, and Shonsey, a slender, blond-haired fella, stumbled out. Laughing and waving his hat as if he'd just heard the most hilarious joke, he lurched over to the hitching post where the group of horses was tied. He saw Thad as he reached to unwind his reins, and his mood sobered considerable. "What are you lookin' at, Walker?"

Thad pushed his hat back and cocked his head to the right. "Exactly."

Shonsey didn't seem to know what to do with that answer. He frowned and gathered up his reins. Behind him, Trampas, followed by hands Frank Canton, Fred Coates, Joe Elliott, and Billy Lykins, stumbled out.

Trampas's gaze bounced back and forth between Shonsey and Thad. His face clouded and he steadied his gait. "There a problem here, Shonsey?" he asked, shooting Thad an unfriendly look.

"No." Shonsey didn't sound convinced, but then shook his head. "Nope." He swung up in the saddle and addressed Thad. "Is there?"

"No," Thad waved away their concerns, "just thought it was funny to see all you boys riding together. Don't any of you have work to do for your bosses?"

"Who says we're not workin'?" Trampas spit a chaw of tobacco at Bo's feet and swung into the saddle. He backed away from the hitching post and pulled up beside Thad. Grinning and showing teeth swimming in tobacco juice, he chuckled. "We got ranch business over close to Buffalo. Reckon somebody like you wouldn't have the stomach for it."

"Headin' off to shoot somebody in the back or maybe lynch a woman?"

The smile melted off Trampas's face like ice cream on a July afternoon. "Why don't you ask your pa about my orders?"

Something snapped in Thad. The ropes holding his patience and good sense—which had been under too much strain lately—broke. Thad launched from his horse, like he was strapped to a rocket, and slammed into Trampas. The two men hit the cold, hard ground with a bone-jarring thud, and Thad went to swinging. A frightening fury erupted in his soul... and his fists. He hammered Trampas's face several times before the man managed his first punch. Trampas delivered a solid strike to Thad's kidney and the pain doubled him over for an instant. The foreman scrambled away as Thad staggered to his feet.

The stab of pain only stoked the fire. Thad was angry, feeling more than a little betrayed, and desperately wanted to share his fine mood. Trampas was the lucky recipient. Thad charged at the foreman, and the two went down again. Dirt and dust wafted up.

Now men had gathered on the walk in front of the saloon. Thad could hear them cheering and jeering as he and his foreman wrestled like snakes and exchanged blows.

"We ain't got time for this, Trampas," Shonsey yelled as the two men rolled beneath his horse, spooking it. The animal pranced and spun, and Shonsey cursed as he fought to rein it in. "I mean it, knock it off!"

Thad and Trampas, clutching each other, punching ribs, kidneys, stomachs, worked their way to their feet. Thad managed to push the other man off and took another blow to the kidney for the effort. He grunted, but the white-hot pain sharpened his anger to a more fierce point. He pulled back a bloody hand and swung at Trampas, nailing him in the jaw with a good, solid blow. Trampas's head snapped back. He staggered, shook his head, and wiped at the blood seeping from his mouth.

Thad took an instant to survey the crowd. He caught Shonsey nodding at someone—

What felt like a hammer blow into his right side stunned Thad. Almost simultaneously, a kick buckled his knees, and he went down hard. Blows rained on his head and ribs. Thad couldn't tell who or how many had jumped into the fray. The punches came from every direction. Pain, black and deep, erupted all over his body. The back of his head, his mouth, his ribs burned.

Getting pummeled, he tried for his feet, but a blow knocked him on his face. Writhing in the cold dirt, he could make out legs and boots. The crowd grew quiet as the punches turned to kicks. The agony in his ribs stole his breath.

"That's enough."

Shonsey.

Thad pawed the ground and managed to get on all fours. He wished he could find Trampas, but more kicks dropped him back to the earth.

"That's enough, I said! We ain't got time for this."

The kicks stopped. Thad lay there, face down in the dirt, blind and breathless with misery. His whole body screamed with raw pain. He barely heard the soft thud of boots and the squeak of leather as the cowboys mounted, then the pounding of hooves as they rode away. A wave of nausea rolled over him and he groaned.

He had to get to his feet.

Thad shook his head and made one more attempt to stand. A hand slipped beneath his arm and lifted him. He recognized the smell of Sheriff Phillips's putrid liniment and, for a moment, thought the stink would cause him to vomit. He stanched the urge and tried to focus, but his vision was fuzzy.

"Come on, son, let's get you cleaned up." The two men slowly limped along the street. "I tell ya, Thad, you were whoopin' the tar outta Trampas, but those other three hit ya from behind. Mighty unsportin' of 'em."

"Yeah, mighty." Thad was surprised at the muffled quality of his own voice. He sounded drunk, or like he'd stuffed cotton in his mouth. Maybe both. His mouth beat like a drum at a pow-wow.

"You want to press charges?"

Pain hummed in every fiber of every muscle. Walking, even slowly, made his ribs feel like they'd been rubbed with kerosene and lit afire. He spat out some blood before answering the sheriff. "Gimmee me thum time to think about it."

"All right. Doc's over toward Buffalo today, but he leaves me a key for instances just like this. Let's go see how much damage those boys did."

❦

Thad wished he could take a bath in the witch hazel. It cooled his ribs right smart and made his busted lip feel a whole lot better. He imagined he could feel the swelling going down.

Sitting on Doc's examination table, he was surprised at Phillips's ability to play doctor, though the man didn't exactly have a gentle touch. He dabbed at Thad's lip one last time, then passed the bottle to him. "Here, I ain't your nurse. You can take over now."

Thad nodded. He took the bottle and a metal bowl of cotton balls and limped over to the sink. His reflection in the mirror made him flinch. He resembled the remains of something trampled by a herd of wild horses. A red swollen eye, puffy purple lip, and bruised cheeks testified to the fight. A lovely assortment of purple and blue bruises peppered his ribs. He couldn't help but wonder what Trampas looked like.

"I was about to stop the fight, in case you was wonderin'."

Thad moved his head a little so he could see the sheriff in the mirror. The big man stood at the door, hands hooked on his suspenders, staring through the glass at the street.

Pa had a habit of standing that same way, and all the lies and turmoil of the last few months hit Thad again. Busted up as he felt, inside and out, he supposed the first thing he should do was what he came into Misery for in the first place.

"Sheriff, that boy that works for Raney—Greg—he has a sister. Do you know where she's at?"

"She better be working at the Golden Lady. Otherwise, the fella that paid me—" Sheriff Phillips nipped that, but Thad heard the worry.

"Otherwise, the fella that paid you to find her might not be happy if he finds out you don't know where she's at."

"Yeah, well, maybe." The sheriff kicked at something then came back with a defensive tone. "Her brother said that's where she's a-workin'. Why would he lie about that instead of saying she worked in a nice place?"

Why, indeed? Thad racked his brain as he wiped away blood and dabbed at bruises, trying to recall everything Grace and Greg had said about Bull. Nothing helped him piece the puzzle together. At least one thing was clear: Grace was hiding from Bull. Thad would do his part to make sure the man never found her. If the sheriff didn't know where she was, Bull would have a hard time finding her.

Thad wiped a cotton ball over his knuckles and let the witch hazel burn and heal. "How'd you even get hooked up with somebody like Bull Hendrick?"

"Who?" The sheriff spun and hooked his thumbs in his belt loops. "Oh, you mean the gal's husband? Bull. That his name? Always signs the telegrams B. Hendrick." He reached up and scratched his head. "I don't rightly know. The gal just come paradin' into my office one mornin' and says, all high-and-mighty like, 'My name is Grace Hendrick. Consider me checked in.' Next thing I know, I get a telegram from the family, wanting to know where she's workin'. That took a little work, but Trampas pointed me to the brother."

"Trampas," Thad whispered through clenched teeth.

"Didn't know the kid was working for Raney, though."

Thad didn't really hear that. He fixated on the *consider me checked in*, as if she'd been ordered here. Sighing, he snatched his shirt off the back of a chair and slipped into it stiffly. His ribs were still beating war drums he was sure could be heard over on the Wind River Reservation. "I'd call it a personal favor, Sheriff, if you give the man as little help as possible when he shows up."

"Well, I don't know, son..." Phillips watched eagerly as Thad fished in his pants pocket. "He paid me twenty-five—I mean, fifty—fifty dollars to find her."

"And you don't know where she's at." Thad tossed the sheriff two shiny, gold coins. "There's a hundred. The Golden Lady is all you need to say."

"You'll be sure to tell your pa I'm helping you out?"

Thad snorted in disgust as he marched past the sheriff out onto the boardwalk. Staring down the street to the Number Nine, Trampas's words came back to him.

Why don't you ask your pa about my orders?

"Trampas and Shonsey were going off to cause trouble, Sheriff. I think you ought to ride after 'em."

"That mean you want to press charges?" The gloom in the sheriff's voice was almost comical.

"Yes, Sheriff, I believe I will." But even as the words left his mouth, Thad knew he was going after the tail of the snake...not the head.

❖

It took Grace a few days to recover from the kick to the ribs. She suspected Raney didn't want her up and around more because a little feminine company around the ranch was a welcome change. By the time

Grace was ready to get out of bed, her boss had a surprise for her.

Turning side to side, Grace appraised her reflection in the oval mirror even as Raney finished buttoning the dress. Red check gingham with long sleeves and a stitched bodice, it wasn't fancy, and the skirt was too wide for the times, but it fit better than the oversized garb she'd been wearing for a month now. Grace had forgotten she had any curves. Stuck in that bed for two days, she thought she was nothing but bruises.

"Glad I saved these," Raney mused. "They're a little out of fashion, but at least they're not pants."

Grace fluffed the skirt and then touched her short hair, barely covering her ears now. She wore it slicked down and parted on the side, the most masculine style she could manage. Still, Grace could see the feminine aspects of her face. Everyone else could only see the boy in her. Funny how Susanna had spotted the lie right off.

"Now, there," Raney chuckled as she surveyed Grace's figure in the mirror. "Oh, my...obviously, you ain't a boy. And I feel pretty stupid."

What was it Susanna had said? "No one was looking for a girl."

"I reckon." Raney began running her fingers through Grace's hair, flipping it and fluffing it, giving her a softer, more feminine edge. "There. That's some better anyway."

"You...you...?"

Both women gasped and spun at the sound of Thad's voice. He stood stock-still, face frozen in horror, lips fighting a grimace. But his *eyes*, wide and haunted, moved. His gaze raced over every inch of Grace, then ricocheted back and forth between her and Raney. Grace wasn't sure what scared her more: his battered face or the curl in his lip.

"Uh oh," the older woman whispered. "Maybe I should go in the kitchen."

"No," Grace and Thad both said in desperate unity.

Grace reached back and grabbed Raney's hand. "No." Her heart galloped in her chest like stampeding cattle.

Thad's expression slowly began to change into something else, something darker. Grace saw the storm forming and felt sick to her stomach. The muscles in Thad's face hardened like iron, his nostrils flared. His blue eyes deepened to a dark, angry purple.

"You've been lying, too."

The resentment and disappointment in his voice broke Grace's heart. "Thad, I can explain." She took a step forward but he stepped back, as if she were carrying the plague.

"All those things I said," he stared at her feet, shaking his head in disbelief. "Telling Greg how I was gonna marry you and how I felt about you." His gaze streaked up. "We slept in the same bed. Went swimmin'...." All the ways Grace had betrayed him. "And it was you the whole time."

"Thad, I'm sorry, but I have a reason for ly—"

"She was only trying to get her son back," Raney jumped in. "You have to believe—"

"Believe?" he spat the word through clenched teeth, and Grace and Raney recoiled. His lip curled into a sneer. "I've got nothin' left to believe in."

Grace wilted beneath his glare. She pressed a hand to her breast, stunned at the depth of her heartbreak.

"I came to tell you that Bull is in town lookin' for you. He shouldn't be able to find you." Thad's tone was as cold as his stare was empty. "At least not easily." He shifted to Raney. "I had a run-in with Trampas, Shonsey, and some hands from a few other outfits." He hung his head and cleared his throat. "I think they're going after somebody. You might want to warn the independents. I'd start with Nate."

Thad raised his hand and rested it on his gun. Moving like he was lifting a huge weight, his head came up, and he locked eyes with Grace. His lips narrowed, the muscles in his neck tightened. Grace wanted to scream she was sorry, beg his forgiveness, but the cold in his expression held her back. "I can't abide a liar."

His words knocked the air out of her, as surely as if he'd kicked her. Jaw clenched like he was biting down on a bullet, he backed through the doorway, disappearing down the hallway. A moment later, the front door slammed shut.

Heartsick, Grace sagged against Raney. "What have I done?"

"You have humiliated a Walker," she sounded as if she'd pronounced a death sentence, "but we can't worry about that now." She took hold of Grace's shoulders and spun her around. "Listen to me carefully. I need you to send a telegram for me. I'll ride over to Nate's to let him know about Trampas and Shonsey so he can warn the other independents." Her gaze drifted. "Then I'm going to the Lazy H to see if I can stop this madness. I'll be back in a day or two."

"All right." Grace knew this was all beyond her petty, broken heart. She could wallow in self-pity later. "I'll hurry."

Raney squeezed Grace's shoulder. "Change back into your old clothes, and keep an eye out for that husband of yours."

"Yes, ma'am."

Chapter Twenty-Six

※◆※

T had was so angry he wanted to shake his fist at Heaven and beat the life out of something. Instead, he and Bo pounded across the sea of brittle, tawny grass like Hell was on his heels.

And it felt like it was.

His whole world was coming undone.

Furious he was even having such melodramatic thoughts, he hunkered down in the saddle and gave Bo his head. The Walkers would stand together and face the WSGA. He would push Pa to do the right thing and quit blaming all the rustling on the independents. He would *make* him see the senseless greed behind all these murders.

And he would never see Grace Hendrick again.

The crack of a rifle from somewhere behind Thad shattered his wallow in self-pity. He reined Bo in and spun him around, pulling his .45 at the same time.

Several hundred yards off, Nick rode toward him, hellbent-for-leather and waving his rifle. Thad kicked Bo into a gallop and cut the distance.

"Hey, brother." Nick hailed him as they both skidded to a stop. "I got some new—" Nick whistled in awe. "What train did you step in front of?"

Thad tightened the reins, pulling his horse's head down and turning him in circles. "Never mind. What's your news?"

Nick holstered the rifle. "The SGA *commissioned* Shonsey and Trampas to do some killin'. They're an honest-to-God assassination squad, and top of their list is Nate Champion. But their first kill was Waggoner."

"You got proof?"

"No, at least not yet, but I trust the information. And, Thad"—Nick licked his lips—"Pa voted for it. He knows what they're doing and who they're going after."

Bo settled down and Thad tried to deal with the miserable, stinking revelation. Paying dues didn't include murdering men who were only trying to make a living. How...? Why had Pa gone so far down this road?

"I'm not the Christian man you are, Thad, but I can't stand by and let this happen. We should have started pushing back when they lynched Ella."

Thad leaned his head back and watched the roiling gray clouds overhead. He felt the same way, churned up and chaotic. "We'll start with Pa. The minute he gets back."

The air in Misery seemed electrified. Tension vibrated all around. As Grace and Dandy trotted down the street, she noticed men running, gathering in small groups, and whispering in the shadows.

Cross looks and fearful expressions collided. A fight broke out in front of the bank, and she had to jerk Dandy to the right to avoid the two men. Fists flying, blood spattering, they called each other names like *dirty independent* and *filthy, boot-licking coward*. It reminded Grace of a fight on the playground. If only the bloodlust over cows and grass were that trivial.

Aware she was riding up the fuse of a powder keg, she kicked Dandy up to an easy lope and hurried toward the Western Union office. She'd promised Raney she would get in and get out, and she planned to keep her word.

Bull grabbed Sheriff Phillips's shirt with big, bulky fingers and shoved the man up against the wall. A deputy reached for his side-arm, but Lonnie drew his slender .32 before the lawman cleared leather.

Pointing at the deputy's heart, Lonnie shook his head. "That would be a bad decision on yer part, mate."

The deputy eased the .45 back into his holster and raised his hands. Trouble in-hand, Bull returned his attention to the sheriff. "Now, I simply need to know why you have been filling my telegrams with this rot about a brother. I need to find my wife." He slammed the sheriff against the wall again and raised his voice to a gravelly yell, "And I need to find her now!"

Sheriff Phillips raised his hands and shook his head. "Honest, mister, I got no idea. She came in, told me her name, then twirled outta here, and that's the last I saw of her."

Bull's hand moved to the sheriff's portly neck. "Maybe you cowboys think we're a couple of dumb city boys, but I will kill you deader than four o'clock, Sheriff—"

"There he is, there he is," the deputy yelled, pointing over Bull's shoulder. "He's right there." Bull dragged the sheriff to the window for a better view. "Yeah, that's the kid brother, Greg."

"Now, this is certainly an interesting development, as my wife does not have a brother."

Phillips's eyes widened. "He—he's been going around tellin' everybody he's her brother."

Bull's gaze ricocheted back and forth from *Greg* to the sheriff. Finally, he released the lawman and smoothed out his filthy, wrinkled shirt. "Well, we'll just go see for ourselves. No hard feelin's, Sheriff?"

The man shook his head energetically to the point Bull thought his jowls created a draft. He snapped his fingers at Lonnie and his man lowered the .32. He did not, however, holster it until he and Bull were on the street. From the shadows of the boardwalk, they watched Grace's *brother* hurry into the Western Union office.

Bull scratched his chin. In the baggy clothes and big hat the kid wore, a resemblance was difficult to nail. Yet, there *was* something familiar about the boy. The way he'd moved, fists tight and held at his side.

Grace did that same thing when she was nervous.

"Lonnie, step back inside and ask our sheriff where this young man works." Lonnie started to move, but Bull put a hand on his chest. "And tell him we'll be needing the use of these fine mounts." He motioned to the bay and roan, saddled up in front of the Sheriff's office.

Lonnie nodded and headed back in to visit once more with the Sheriff of Misery.

❦

Grace loped across the empty hills, trying to outrun all these twisted emotions. Her heart felt like a wagon load of barbed wire, a tangled mess of sharp, painful edges.

There wasn't a horse in the world fast enough, so she slowed Dandy to a walk.

The fury in Thad's eyes when he'd realized the lie —she flinched merely recalling it. He hated her, and the realization left her bleeding. How could it hurt so much?

And then she'd had to send Raney's telegram to Katie. Salt in the wound.

Angry with herself for being so foolish, Grace tugged Dandy to a stop. Her throat hurt from holding in a sob. If she could just see Hardy, she could bear all this other turmoil and walk away from it. But the *what-ifs* rained down on her like brimstone. What if Bull had found out about the telephone call? What if he'd already shipped Hardy off to some boarding school in Europe? What if he was on his way to kill her?

What if Thad never spoke to her again?

Sniffling and batting her lashes, she tried to hold back tears, but they spilled down her cheeks. The infinite Wyoming expanse wavered like a mirage.

What if she never saw her son again?

The possibility terrified her. She hated Bull so much. She hated this inability to get to her son. She hated carrying this burden alone.

"Oh, God," she whispered, desperate to reach Him, desperate to be heard. She considered the boundless, wide horizon and wondered if there really was a great Being seated on a throne, Someone Who cared about her and her son. "Please, if You're there, please help me. I've made such a mess of things. I know I can't have Thad, but please, if I can just get my son back..."

She waited a few moments, but no great revelation warmed her soul, no angelic choir filled the sky. Instead, the cold and lonely reality settled into her bones as the wind numbed her ears.

Swallowing the agonizing disappointment and wondering what she had expected anyway, she clutched the reins and moved to kick Dandy when motion about a mile off caught her eye.

Men, on horseback. Five of them, moving at a lope or canter. Not in a hurry, but not dillydallying either. They rode with obvious intention, headed toward Buffalo, maybe?

And she couldn't have cared less.

A steady snow had settled in, and a sharp wind was biting like a mountain lion by the time Grace topped the last hill above Raney's. Her fingers and toes were numb, and her ears and nose were burning, but she was happy to see light glowing in the windows and smoke chugging from the chimney. A hot cup of coffee never sounded so good. Kicking Dandy up to a canter, she hurried on in.

Stripping the horse down and readying her for a night in the stall seemed an interminable task, but Grace finally closed the stall gate and jogged over to the house.

She pushed the door open. "Raney, I'm back!" Grace stomped the snow off her boots then stepped inside. "I'm surprised you beat me. Please say you've got some coffee on the stove." Grace started peeling out of her coat. "Raney?"

The woman didn't answer and Grace paused, the coat hanging on one arm. The house was too quiet. And something *felt*...wrong. A pot clanged in the kitchen, and she breathed a sigh of relief. Maybe Raney was boiling water and simply hadn't heard—

"Hello, Grace."

Bull's mass filled the doorway to the kitchen, and Grace's knees nearly buckled. She had to grab the hall-tree to keep from falling. "What are you doing here? How did you find me?"

Bull raised a steaming cup of coffee, took a sip, and smacked his lips with satisfaction. "Mmmm, that is good on a cold night." He cocked his head to one side. "But it's no substitute for you, dear."

Grace straightened, a bluff to cover her shock and crushing despair at the sight of him. Should she run? An irrational thought since she didn't know where she would run to. Perhaps Bull was just checking on her. Her current vocation certainly was not going to sit well with him, though, and she knew it.

The thought drained away her fear and filled the void with hate, black and rich like the oil pit on the North Forty. He would never leave her alone. Never give her any peace. Even after shipping her off to Wyoming, his maniacal quest for control had forced him to follow her here.

"Ah, Grace, I always could read you like a book." He tossed his cup to the floor, shattering it and sending coffee splattering everywhere. "I know you hate me." He raised a black eyebrow. "In a way, I hate you, too. You're my wife. I own you. And you've made a fool of me." A flush crept into his cheeks. A vein bulged in his neck. The signs his anger was growing. "You wanted to act like a whore back in Chicago. I couldn't have that. Remember, you were supposed to be my *respectable* wife." He flexed his fist. "But, here, in the land of cowboys and cattle, why, if it was a whore you wanted to be, I thought I'd oblige."

His face hardened and he took a step toward her. Grace pulled the .44 from her hip, steady and smooth, like oil pouring from a bottle. Bull's eyes bulged. She relished the turn of events. For once, *he* could stare down the barrel of a gun. She cocked it, and the sound was deafening. "I hate you, Bull, with every square inch of my soul."

"It takes a lot of hate to kill a man, Grace. You got it in you?"

Grace didn't move, didn't breathe. She let the steadiness of her arm answer his question.

Almost as if he was bored and merely going through the motion, Bull casually raised his hands. "No one has ever pulled a gun on me and lived to tell about it, Grace." He pointed at her. "But you'll be the exception. Do you know why?"

Her finger tightened on the trigger. She could pull it and be free of this monster. "Why?"

"Because to let you live will be a greater punishment."

She smelled Lonnie before she saw him, but she saw him too late. He shoved the Smith & Wesson up against her temple and wrenched the revolver out of her hand before she could blink. Just like that, the balance of power shifted back to Bull.

He walked up to Grace and cupped her chin. "Go quietly, and maybe I'll let you see Hardy before I ship him off to Switzerland. Give me any trouble, and I'll not only get rid of him *before* we get back to Chicago," he surveyed the room, "but we'll wait around long enough to kill the old widow lady and throw her body to the coyotes." He shoved a thumb into his armpit and tried to affect a mocking cowboy accent. "I hear thar's lots of dangerous varmints in these parts, ma'am."

Burning with the hate that would have allowed one

fateful twitch of a finger, Grace shook her head. "I'm the only one you'll have to worry about."

Bull and Lonnie hee-hawed like mules over the suggestion. Suddenly, she saw the flash of his fist and felt the stars of pain explode in her head. Her mouth filled with the coppery taste of warm blood as she staggered back. Bull grabbed her collar and pulled her to him. "Welcome back to the fold, Grace."

Chapter Twenty-Seven

❧❧❧

T had and Nick stopped at the entrance to their father's study. The door was cracked open several inches. Pa sat quietly at his desk, writing and sipping a brandy.

As if nothing in the world is wrong.

Thad realized he didn't know the man anymore. Somewhere along the way, he'd become so obsessed with regaining Pa's trust that he'd gone blind to the greed consuming him. Probably, Pa hadn't seen it either.

None of that mattered now.

"Pa," he and Nick pushed through the doors and marched up to his desk, "we have to talk."

Pa set down the fountain pen and leaned back in his chair. With a casual air, he surveyed Thad from head to toe. "You been scrappin' with a bobcat?"

"I ran into Shonsey and Trampas in town."

Pa responded with a raised eyebrow. "And?"

"It wasn't the day to push me." He clenched his

jaw and leaned in. "Trampas said he had ranch business. Business I wouldn't have the stomach for. But he said I could ask *you* about his orders." Thad took a deep breath and dropped his hands on his hips. "Say it straight up. Did you vote for the assassination squad?"

Pa rubbed his chin and eyed his boys. "That what they're calling it?"

Thad and Nick answered with stoic silence.

"I take it you don't agree with this stand?"

"Pa," Nick edged closer to him, "we ain't murderers. I won't be a party to this."

"Neither will I." Thad ground his teeth. "It's wrong."

"Well, aren't you two a pretty pair of hypocrites? Long as the trouble stays down in Natrona County, you're happy to bury your heads in the sand." Pa sniffed and then took a slow sip of brandy. After a moment, he rose to his feet, towering over his boys.

Neither son bowed. Those days were gone, but Pa didn't seem to know it.

"Boys, I run this ranch as I see fit. Until such time as you take over, or I am dead, you will go along with my decisions."

"No, sir, we won't." Thad glanced at Nick, who nodded in agreement. "We're not sanctioning murder. We don't want any truck with that."

Pa's cheeks flushed crimson, and he slammed his fist down on the desk. "I said I'd keep you out of it. You're not involved."

"We are involved!" Thad fired back. "We're not burying our heads in the sand anymore, Pa. You aren't the judge, and the SGA isn't the jury. The intimidation, the killin', it all has to stop!"

"Killin' and dyin' is life in Wyoming!" Pa thundered. "Only the strong survive here."

"So Maggie and Bill..." Thad purposely gentled his voice. "They weren't strong enough, is that it?"

Pa's mouth slammed shut, but his eyes blazed. Thad couldn't feel the heat anymore. The truth was the only thing that could cause him pain now. "You wanted his land, so you figured to get it by taking the thing most precious to him?"

"And what about the Bar T and Box S?" Nick shook his head in disgust. "Those weren't accidents, either, were they?"

"Now ask him about the Diamond R...and Jake."

Raney's soft but steely voice sliced into their conversation like a knife. Pa's gaze shot past his sons, and the color drained from his face. Thad and Nick turned.

She stood in the entrance, shoulders bowed under the weight of Wyoming's *dues*. Her brown eyes faded to the tint of winter wheat and glistened with tears. She approached Pa slowly, her steps halting and unsteady. Her gaze bored into him. Thad could sense the panic coming off his father in waves.

"Look me in the eye, Earl, and tell me about Jake's death."

Pa sat down hard. "I don't know anything about his death."

Raney's face sagged as if the denial broke her heart. "It all started when Lucille died, didn't it?" She wrung her hands and worried her bottom lip. "I didn't put everything together until I was riding back from Nate's."

She spoke softly, reasoning aloud, and Thad figured at least some of the story of Raney and Pa would finally come out. Faced with it, he wasn't sure he wanted any more truth.

"I know you married her to get back at me for choosin' Jake, but you came to love her." Raney whipped her head up. "Boys, believe me, he loved your ma more than he ever loved me." She drifted back to him. "And I guess she was the last thing standing between you and your ambition." Pain creased her brow, sadness pulling the corners of her mouth down.

Pa stared back at her, stony, unflinching.

The difference in their expressions struck Thad.

"They went for Nate Champion today." Raney gave him a moment to consider that. "Came so close, he's got a powder burn on his cheek."

Desperate to move, to feel like he was more than a bystander in this drama, Thad gently touched Raney's elbows and guided her to the chair in front of Pa's desk. She sat, patted his hand on her shoulder, and spoke to Pa with a stronger voice. "Nate's goin' after them. He saw Trampas and Shonsey and can identify 'em. It'll trace straight back to you and the SGA."

Thad stood behind Raney and wondered about her earlier comment. *I didn't put everything together until I was riding back from Nate's.* "What did you put together, Raney?"

She kept her gaze on Pa. "Trampas."

A memory struck Thad and he leaned toward Pa. "You hired him the day after Jake was killed."

Raney nodded. "And in just a couple of years, how many of your neighbors moved away or sold you their land? How many accidents happened on their spreads?" Her voice began to rise. "How many families slipped away in the night because they were afraid of winding up like Ella?" Her bottom lip quivered. "How many widows have you made in this county?" Raging like a tornado, she leaped to her feet and swept everything on Pa's desk to the floor, then slammed her hands down in front of him. "Tell me the truth about Jake!" Her voice choked with fury. "Tell me! Did Trampas kill him? Or was it you?"

"It was an accident," Pa screamed back at her, leaping to his feet. "I swear to God it was an accident."

The confession stilled the room. It hung in the air thick and suffocating like a shroud.

Enraged, Thad wanted to choke the life out of his father, but he waited, instead, for Raney's reaction.

She pulled back and whispered, "Earl, what have you done?"

Pa collapsed into his chair. Emotions rolled across his face, but regret was the last to settle as he recalled a dark moment. "I'd been drinking, my pitiful attempt to deal with Lucille's death. I came across Jake out ridin' your fence. I was angry and sick with grief. And guilt." He rested his elbows on the desk and rolled his head from side to side. "I told him you still loved me. I just wanted him to hurt like I was hurting." He swallowed and fought for control of his voice. "We got into it." Pa scrubbed a hand over his face as if wishing he could wipe away the memories. "My God, Raney, I'm sorry. He hit me, and I knew he'd beat the hound out of me. I don't even remember goin' for my gun."

Thad and Nick both took a step back, horror-stricken. For years, Thad had believed the lie that Jake was probably killed by rustlers, that he'd stumbled on them in the middle of trying to steal his cattle. And all along...

He turned his back on Pa and fought to loosen the knot in his throat. Soul-deep grief wrestled with fury. Everything he'd believed about his father was a lie. Lies, lies, and more lies. He couldn't stomach them anymore.

"Trampas saw the whole thing." His father's second confession shocked Thad almost as much as the first, and he spun back around. Pa shook his head. "I made him foreman. He said he'd keep his mouth shut, but he kept pushing for more, getting me in deeper. Folks kept abandoning their spreads." He shrugged weakly. "Opportunities presented themselves..." he trailed off.

Nick's face contorted into an expression of anguish and rage. Sneering, he leaned over to their father. "You've built this ranch on the blood of your neighbors. Keep it."

He spun and started to storm out, but Thad grabbed his arm. "Nick, wait." He reached down and gently grasped Raney's shoulder. "Raney, you need three good hands, don't you?"

"Wait, what?" Pa stood. "What do you think you're doin'?"

"For one thing, Pa, we're going to the sheriff. And if Phillips doesn't arrest you and Trampas and the others, I'll contact a federal marshal." Slowly, he lifted

Raney to her feet. "In the meantime, we'll get the Diamond R back into production." He smiled at her, though there wasn't any joy behind it.

Raney gave him a slight, stiff nod.

Thad swung back to Pa, hoping to show only his defiance, not his pain. "Nick, Adam, and I will take our cut from the herd, but no matter how things flush out...I ain't ever coming back here."

※

Thad slapped the porch post, frustrated by this life of lies. "Raney, I was just runnin' off at the mouth in there. I don't know if you want to bring the Diamond R back into production or not, but we're gettin' our cattle off the Lazy H."

Biting her bottom lip, she drifted over and sat down in Pa's rocking chair. Thad would swear she'd aged ten years in the last ten minutes. Everything about her, from hunched shoulders to grooved brow, spoke of weariness.

Nick sat down on the bench beside her and absently twirled his hat as he spoke, staring at nothing. "Raney, I'm not staying here. I'm done with the Lazy H. If you want our help, you've got all three of the Walkers. Otherwise, we'll pay you to use your land."

"If that isn't irony for you," she mumbled, staring out at the Big Horn Mountains. Chuckling, she came back to Nick and touched his hand. "Your ma would be proud of you two." A deep V formed in her brow, and she stood again, albeit slowly and stiffly. "You can't walk away from this ranch. It's your legacy."

Thad leaned against the post and shook his head. "Too much of it's been built on blood money, Raney. I can't live with that."

"Me neither." Nick ran his hand through his hair and slipped his hat back on as he stood. "Adam will feel the same way. We'll have to make things right with the folks Pa stole from—" He flinched and dipped his head. "At least we'll do the best we can. We'll give you back the land he bought from ya after Jake's death—"

"Boys," Raney reached out and clutched Nick's hand then Thad's. "We can't fix everything right now. Maybe not at all, I don't know. Right now, I just want to get home and think on all this. Greg should be back and we'll—"

"*Grace*." Thad spat, pulling his hand from Raney's. Nick backed up at the venom in his brother's tone. "You mean *Grace*. What are you gonna do with her?"

Raney frowned hard at him. "Thad, you are one of the kindest, wisest, most sober young men I know. But, just like all men," she cast a glance toward the house, "and especially Walker men, your pride makes you stupid." She stepped over to him and poked him in the chest. "That girl did what she thought she had to do to get back to her *son*." She pointed a thumb at herself. "I admire her sand. And I hope she stays...or gets her son and comes back. I was thinkin' of makin' her a partner, but, well..." She looked around the porch and sighed, "reckon we'll hammer all that out."

Thad studied the house he was preparing to leave and nodded. "All right. Fine. Nick, Trampas gets wind of all this trouble we're fixin' to bring down on Pa and the SGA, he'll either leave the country or try to kill us."

Nick nodded as he marched down the porch steps to his horse tied beside Raney's. "You thinkin' we need to go after him?"

"I don't know. Maybe. I'll get Raney home safe then ride in and see the sheriff. You fetch Adam. Meet me back at her place."

"Brother, I don't think you need to ride for the sheriff alone."

"Nick, *Adam* is alone, and he doesn't know about Trampas."

Nick understood. He nodded and swung into his saddle. "You be careful, then."

⁂

Thad walked in behind Raney and stomped over to her *cold* fireplace. Some hand *Greg* was. Had *she* let the kitchen stove go out as well? Fuming, he commenced tossing logs into the fireplace. Raney needed a fire going before he headed into Misery.

The ride over from the Lazy H had been long, silent, and cold as the two of them wrangled with the lies and the revelations. He felt a desperate need to pray but had to make sure Raney and Greg—*Grace*— were safe. He flinched at the slip and promised himself someday he'd give *Grace* a piece of his mind. If she wanted to act like a man, maybe she should take a cussin' like a man.

In need of kindling, he rose and headed toward the kitchen. "Raney, I—" he stopped mid-sentence. She stood near the stove, staring down at something on the floor. Her tense shoulders and perfect stillness sliced him with dread.

Grace?

Stunned at the tidal wave of fear flooding through him, he rushed to Raney and skidded to a stop. She bent down and came back up with a half-smoked cigar and a piece of a broken mug. Shards of the cup and coffee littered her floor. "He found her. Somehow, he found her."

Chapter Twenty-Eight

"You have to go after her."

Thad marched back to the fireplace and shoved his handful of kindling beneath the logs. "What am I supposed to do, Raney? Kidnap her away from her own husband?"

"Yes!"

"You know I can't do that." Even if he could muster past his wounded pride, how was he supposed to justify to God the stealing of another man's wife? "Besides"— he struck a match and put it to the pine branch— "they've got a son. I can't come between that."

"He's using the son as leverage."

Thad worked with the fire a moment, made sure it caught, and then squatted on his haunches. "What do you mean, leverage?"

Raney sat down on the stone hearth. "He banished her here, Thad, and told her if she came back to Chicago or tried to get to their son, he'd send him away to boarding school. She'd never see him again. He picked Misery 'cause he figured she'd"—Raney rubbed her hands together nervously—"well...choose to do anything but starve."

She clutched Thad's arm, but he wouldn't look away from the fire. He wished the flames would burn off his confusion...and hurt. Grace had lied to him. Over and over. Brazenly.

"But she didn't."

Thad had lost track of Rainey's point. "Didn't what?"

She huffed with frustration. "Grace beat him. She found a way to survive without...selling herself." She stood and turned to the fire as well. "And now he's here. I don't think it's because he missed her smiling face. And I'm afraid for her."

Thad's heart swung violently between wanting to murder Grace and murder for her. He simply couldn't corral all these emotions. Done listening to Raney hammer away at her fears, he jumped up and started for the door.

"Where are you going?"

He stopped with his hand on the knob. Just where the heck *was* he going? He couldn't think. He'd been fed enough lies for the last month—shoot, the last three years—to choke a mule. And now he had this sick feeling about Grace that fought to outweigh all of it...but he wouldn't let it. "I'm going to see the sheriff, like I planned."

"She needs you, Thad."

Incredulous, he spun around. "She lied to me,

Raney. Made a complete fool out of me. You just expect me to go chasing after her?"

She stormed across the room. "I expect you to save her."

"From her *husband*? Well, it ain't gonna happen."

"Why? Because of your pride?" She stabbed his chest once more, wearing a scowl worthy of Pa. "Let me tell you about pride. It makes you walk away from people you should run toward. It makes you marry the wr—" Her voice broke, and her chin quivered. Eyes filling with tears, she looked away and sniffled.

Thad had never seen Raney like this and didn't know what to make of it. Was she still in love with Pa? He was in way over his head with all these emotions and wanted to run. Instead, he cowboyed up and squeezed her shoulder with a gloved hand. "Raney, she did marry the wrong man. And I can't—" Emotion tangled his own voice. Again, surprised at the turmoil Grace was causing him, he wrestled the feelings down. "She'll put her son first, that much I do know. And if he is using him for leverage, she won't come with me."

"Then figure something out."

Thad raised his face to the ceiling and exhaled deeply, but none of the frustration left him. "I'll talk to the sheriff about her." The promise left him feeling empty. Phillips wouldn't interfere in a bad marriage. "That's all I know to do right now."

Snow pelting his face, the frigid, dark ride into Misery gave Thad plenty of time to sort his thoughts. Or at least he tried to. Funny thing was he kept coming back to Grace.

He should be praying about forgiving his father. Even Trampas. He should be planning his words to the sheriff so the lawman might actually arrest Trampas and the leaders of the SGA. But all he could think about was saving Grace. And the only plan that leaped to mind was flattening Bull and whisking her away.

Chivalrous but stupid. Bull held the leverage because he held her son.

Why had Bull come for her? Just to assess her situation here, or to take her back to Chicago?

Thad realized the snow had stopped and the moonlight was clawing its way through the rolling clouds. The road glowed before him and he kicked Bo into a canter while he had some light.

The desolate, silvery landscape reminded him that he had many a long, cold winter night ahead of him. Who would he spend them with?

A month ago, he thought he knew. Eventually, he'd find the right gal to marry, a gal who loved Wyoming and ranching as much as he did. They'd build their own home over on that butte he'd admired since he was ten. Their children, and maybe even their grandchildren, would grow up on the Lazy H. Yes, indeed, he'd had it all planned out.

Now, he didn't have a clue what tomorrow morning was gonna bring, much less the next year or decade. All his plans, everything he had ever put his faith in, had evaporated—

You know that's not true.

The still, small voice tugged at his soul, and he

nodded. *No, I know You're still here. Things are just so hard right now, Lord, and about as clear as mud. I've never not been able to see where I'm going. Now, I'm turning my own father in to the law, and I'm in love*—he stumbled over the word, evaluated it, and nodded again. *I'm in love with a married woman. Things are upside down.*

Are they? asked the Voice. *And what doth the Lord require of thee, but to do justly, and to love mercy, and to walk humbly with thy God?*

Thad didn't know why the verse from Micah ran through his mind, but it echoed in his brain as the lights of Misery came into view.

...do justly, love mercy, walk humbly...

He trotted through Misery, the town all but asleep. Weak, amber light spilled onto the empty street here and there from quiet homes. Bo's hooves ground through the icy snow, disturbing the pristine silence, and a finger of uneasiness slithered down Thad's backbone. Someone was watching him, or was he just paranoid? Either way, riding right down Main Street was pretty boneheaded. Up ahead, he saw two horses tied outside Phillips's office. He wasn't sure in the low light, but one resembled Nate's appaloosa, and Thad felt better about this course of action. Maybe when Thad chimed in with his information, Champion and the other independents could stop the SGA.

The deadly, metallic click-click of a rifle registered with Thad. He twisted to see behind him. Fire streaked from the shadows. The boom from the gun and the bullet hit him like a sledgehammer. He flipped out of the saddle as Bo screamed and bolted down the street. Thad hit the ground face-first, snow and dirt grinding into his teeth.

Another shot sent a plume of snow into the air right beside his head. He drew his Colt, scrambled to his feet, and fired into the darkness where he'd seen the muzzle flash. Dizzy, he fought to stay upright as the shadows wavered around him like smoke. He blinked, trying to clear his vision, and fired again.

"Thad, over here! I'll cover you, son!"

Pa?

Thad didn't have to hear his father's voice twice. Firing behind him as he ran for the opposite side of the street, he kept low and lunged for Blankenship's Mercantile. Pa fired off to the right, covering his sprint for safety. Thad leaped over a flour barrel like a cougar after a deer, landed on his shoulder, and rolled into the locked front door.

"Thad, you all right? You hit?"

Thad followed the voice down the boardwalk. A rifle barrel waved at him from behind a wagon, and he caught the silhouette of Pa's big-brimmed Stetson.

"Yeah." His side burned and throbbed, declaring his injury. Pa cursed. Thad touched the warm, sticky spot just below his ribs and prayed it wasn't too bad. "Yeah, I'm hit."

Across the street, the door to the jail flew open, spilling light onto the street. "Who's out there?" Nate called from inside the doorway.

Thad crawled over to the barrel and peered around it. "It's me, Nate. Thad Walker. I got Pa with me."

Nate seemed to ponder that. "You here for me?"

Thad cast a quick glance toward his father. "No...

I'm here to turn Pa in. I thought you were going after Trampas and Shonsey."

"I thought I'd better let a few people know where I was headin', 'case I didn't come back."

"I can corroborate your story, Nate. I know it was Trampas and Shonsey who attacked you today. Pa was in on the SGA's vote that commissioned them."

Several more seconds ticked by before Nate responded. "I don't think I believe that, Walker. I think you're here to finish it."

"I didn't even know you were in Misery. Besides, if that was the case, why am I the one gettin' shot at?"

"Because your mouth is too big." Trampas's voice and the sound of a gun cocking squeezed Thad's heart. He flinched at the stupidity of letting the man sneak up behind him. "You're not turning your pa in, and you're not turning me in."

"Drop it, Trampas." Pa rose out of the shadows like an avenging angel, his rifle glinting in the weak moonlight. Fury seethed in his voice. "I said drop it, or I will kill you graveyard dead."

Thad almost smiled, comforted to know the old Earl Walker was still alive.

Trampas's eyes darted back and forth from Thad to Pa. "He's going to turn you in, Mr. Walker."

Thad tightened his grip on his gun. His side ached like a mule had kicked him, and he felt light-headed. Trying to shake off the woozy feeling, he readied his weakening muscles to turn and fire. Was he faster than Trampas? He had to be...

"I won't tell you again, boy." Earl moved slowly until he was standing beside Thad. "I've done some terrible things. Letting you kill my son won't be one of 'em."

The moment stretched out. Time lost its meaning as the sky started spitting snowflakes again.

"Not me, Mr. Walker. I'm not swingin' for a bunch of rich, greedy bast—"

In an instant, gunfire lit the night. Thad spun, but Pa stepped in front of him, blocking his view of Trampas. Guns blazed again. Feeling like he was in a sleepy, crazy dream, Thad moved over and fired at Trampas. The foreman fired but twitched and jerked crazily as Thad and Pa emptied their guns into him. A heartbeat later, Trampas slid to the boardwalk in a dark heap.

The overwhelming desire to sleep engulfed Thad. He dropped to his knees and pitched forward, diving into the darkness.

Chapter Twenty-Nine

❦

Bull shoved Grace into the empty train seat, plunking down beside her. Lonnie settled on the bench across from them, wearing that awful leer Grace wished she could claw off his face. The cold ride into town had felt good on her throbbing cheek, but her toes, nearly frozen, burned now as the warmth returned to them.

"Stoke the fire, Lonnie." Bull removed his derby and tossed it to the seat beside his thug. "I need a few moments alone with my lovely bride."

Lonnie nodded and headed to the stove at the front of the empty car. Bull draped his arm around Grace. Trapped like a caged animal, she stiffened but didn't bother to pull away. "Now, darlin', let's square away a few things. Until I decide what to do with you, you don't breathe a word about this charade of yours." He moved his hand to her neck and dug his fingers into her muscle. Grace writhed against the pain and whimpered. "You tried to make a fool of me, and I will

repay you, my lovely"—he put his lips to her ear—
"every day for the rest of your miserable life. But cheer
up"—he pulled away and patted the muscle—"maybe
it won't be that long."

Somewhere off in the distance, gunfire erupted.
Five or six shots...then silence. Lonnie rejoined them
and laughed. "Guess that's what passes for a gunfight
out 'ere in the Wild West, eh?"

Grace saw Bull's smirk reflected in the window.
"Choir practice, compared to Fifteenth Street, huh?"

The whistle blew and the train to Cheyenne
started its long, slow crawl across the prairie. She
craned her neck, watching Misery fade. She wondered
where Thad was. Would he miss her? Would he ever
think of her kindly? Would Raney keep her ranch? She
fought back bitter tears and settled into her seat.

Now, only Hardy mattered.

Clearly, Bull had something awful in store for
Grace. He might even be planning to kill her. She
knew, without a doubt, no matter what hell she had to
walk through, she and Hardy would get away...

Bull's lip lifted in a little sneer, as if he had read her
thoughts. "Say goodbye to Wyoming, dear."

❧

When Thad came to, gunfire echoed in his head, and
he screamed.

"Easy, Thad, easy."

He opened his eyes and followed the hand on his
chest to Raney's face. She sat on the edge of his cot, a
damp cloth in her hand. Relief washed over him and

he settled back. *Everything is all right...* "I got shot. But I'm all right." He looked around the small Spartan examination room. Alcohol and bandages sat on the nightstand next to him, his second round of medical treatment in Doc's office.

"Yesss," Raney dragged out. "Yes, you are."

She might as well have added the *but*. Thad raised an eyebrow at her. "What aren't you telling me?"

"Trampas is dead. Nate rode out lookin' for Shonsey and the others, and we haven't heard anything yet." Her chin quivered and she bit her bottom lip. She took Thad's hand and squeezed it hard. "Thad." Her voice quivered. "I'm so sorry about your pa."

He heard the statement but couldn't glean any understanding. "I don't understand. What about Pa?"

Comprehension dawned on Raney's face. "You don't know. In the gunfight, Trampas shot him...Earl's gone."

❧

Exhausted, filthy, and hungry, Grace stepped down out of the carriage in front of her home—her prison. Nearly midnight, gas torches burned invitingly on each side of the stately oak and iron door, creating such an illusion of security and warmth.

Behind her, the carriage door slammed shut, and she spun.

Peering out the window, Bull tipped his derby. "I've business to attend. Make sure you resemble a woman by the time I get back."

The carriage drove away, and Grace trudged up to

the big, heavy door. Prison or not, Hardy was on the other side. Her feet took flight. She bounded through the quiet, dimly lit foyer and raced up the steps to his room, her cowboy boots thumping loudly on the wooden floor. Holding her breath, she pushed open the door, gasping with delight at the sight of her baby snoozing peacefully in his bed.

Dark curls lay matted against his forehead. Chubby little fingers clutched a stuffed bear. Her throat constricted with joy, and she crept over to him. She kneeled down beside him and gently touched his fingers. Hardy stirred. In the pale moonlight, Grace saw his eyelids flutter open, and he was staring at her with an expression of bewilderment verging on alarm.

"Shhhh, it's all right, Hardy." She clutched his hand. "It's me, Mommy."

He yawned, then suddenly flung back his covers and launched himself into her arms, nearly knocking her down. "Mommy, I knew you'd come back. I knew it!"

Joy, so sublime it seemed almost painful, exploded in Grace's heart, and she hugged Hardy like she was clinging to a life preserver. He squeezed her back so tightly around her neck he nearly constricted the blood flow to her brain. Laughing and crying, Grace wiggled loose and covered Hardy's face in kisses. "Oh, my baby, how I have missed you," she whispered.

"Me, too, Mommy." Hardy hugged her tight again. "Please don't ever leave me again."

The plea broke her heart, and Grace wept into her son's shoulder. "No, baby, don't you worry about that. I'll never, ever leave you again."

"Even when Daddy gets a new wife?"

She stiffened for a moment and then shook her head. Bull's philandering never ceased, and it wouldn't surprise her if he had a *new* respectable wife waiting in the wings. That didn't change the fact that she'd never leave Hardy again. "No matter what Daddy does, Hardy, you and I will never be separated again."

Chapter Thirty

❧

G race absently smoothed her dress down as she perused the books in the library, wishing something as simple as a work of fiction could distract her. It felt so strange to be home, stranger still to be in a dress, even after five days. But Bull had commanded it. Still true to form, he usually came wandering in around noon or so, smelling of liquor, cigars, and perfume.

And always with one thing on his mind. Until she had a plan to get Hardy away from here, she couldn't think of anything to do but play her role as the long-suffering wife.

Bull kept all his money in the safe, and on the train, he'd said she would not be receiving any, even for household expenses, and he had informed her she would be watched around the clock. She felt more trapped than she ever had. But there had to be a way out...

She tried not to think about Thad, but she could

see him clear as day, riding and roping and loving every minute of it. Full of life, in his element on the Lazy H, laughing with his men, cutting up with Raney, and making up nicknames.

She'd never forget him.

Behind her, Hardy started humming *Frère Jacques* as he played with his Lincoln Logs in front of the fire. In her absence, he had become quite adept at building homes. Yesterday, she had helped him build a bunkhouse and told him the story of the fat rattler that had nearly struck her.

Her hand drifted across the Holy Bible, and she thought about the day out on the windswept pasture when she'd begged God for help. She wanted to be angry with Him for denying it but didn't have the energy. She could only love Hardy and hate Bull. There wasn't room for anything—or anyone—else.

Out of sheer hopelessness, she pulled the book from the shelf, opened it, and read the first words she saw.

Fear thou not, for I am with thee: be not dismayed, for I am thy God: I will strengthen thee, yea, I will help thee, yea, I will uphold thee with the right hand of My righteousness.

The scripture seemed so directed at Grace she read it again. And again.

The words rained down on her soul, and she felt an old thirst fading. Peace and comfort filled her up to overflowing. She drifted a finger over the scripture, half-expecting to feel something.

*I am with thee...I will help thee...*echoed over and over in her heart...And she believed the words.

"Grace!"

Bull's bellowing startled both her and Hardy. He looked up with wide, fearful eyes, and her heart broke. He was terrified of his father. Shoving the Bible back onto the shelf, she walked over to him and took his hand. "Hardy, your father and I have some talking to do." She tried to smile. "We won't be long."

Marie stepped into the room and waited by the door. Grace nodded at the nanny and pulled Hardy to his feet. "Why don't you two go upstairs? Sit in that sunny spot in your window and Marie will read *Alice in Wonderland* to you."

"All right. Will you come up when you and Daddy are done talking?"

"I certainly will. I'll read some, too, if you like."

Nodding but moving like he was wading through molasses, Hardy took Marie's hand, and the two slipped out the door. Almost immediately, Bull filled the doorway, leering at Grace, a fresh cigar clenched between his teeth. The stink of whiskey wafted off him. "Your hair is finally getting to a respectable length." He lumbered across the room and grabbed her arm, casting the cigar into the fireplace. "Hike up that skirt, woman." Grace slapped at him as he pawed her, but he intercepted her hand and twisted it behind her back.

"Bull, not here! Have you lost your mind?"

"By God, if I tell you to raise your skirt over your head right in front of the servants, you'll obey me!"

His face darkened as he groped her and attempted to spin her. She realized he was trying to bend her over the writing desk and writhed madly in his arms. She wanted to scream but knew that would bring the servants. He wove his fingers through her hair, below her ears now, and jerked her head back. "You're just giving me an excuse to make it rougher, Grace."

"Tsk, tsk, tsk," Lonnie's slimy voice hissed, pausing Bull's hands. "Marital discord. 'Ow sad."

Bull swung around to the door, still holding Grace by the hair. "I'm busy. Come back later."

"Well, that's the thing of it." Lonnie sauntered into the room, drew his .32, and pointed it at his boss.

Bull's face flushed with fury, his lip curling into a sneer. "You little limey bast—"

"I am a lot of things, but that ain't one of 'em, Bull. My mum was a good woman. Now, my da, 'e was much too much like you. And that's when it came to me."

"What?" Bull growled.

Grace wondered if, by some miracle, Lonnie was here to save her. Her hopes lifted when he cocked the pistol. "The Italians want you out of the way, Bull, and I said I could 'elp with that. Make it look like your wife did it. A service for which they are 'appily going to pay me a tidy sum."

"You won't live to spend it." Bull tightened his grip on Grace. "Besides, Grace won't protect you."

"I thought of that. I thought about using 'Ardy to make her." Lonnie shrugged off the idea. "Ah, but that's messy and leaves loose ends. So I decided to take a lesson from my dear old da. You see, he shot my mum then turned the gun on himself. No loose ends. No one to dispute his story."

Bull's jaw clenched with fury. "What are you saying? You're going to shoot me? Make it look like

Grace did it?" He sounded as if he couldn't believe Lonnie's audacity...or stupidity.

"Ah, you catch on quick. Then I'll kill 'er and put the gun in 'er 'and. *Distraught wife shoots abusive 'usband, then 'erself.* The servants will all verify your treatment of your lovely bride. Personally, I don't know 'ow she's gone this long without shootin' you."

"Lonnie, you can't do this," Grace pleaded. "My son, Hardy..."

"Don't worry, luv, the state will provide the lad a good 'ome."

With that, Lonnie fired his gun. Grace jumped. Her ears rang.

The fury on Bull's face melted into an expression of fear and confusion. His brow dipped and he swayed on his feet. "I didn't think he'd do it—" Suddenly, his breathing hitched oddly. Shaking his head, he let go of Grace's hair, splaying his fingers over his chest and a spreading red stain. Terrified, Grace tried to wiggle free, but Bull held on with a death grip at her wrist. "Shot..." he trailed off and dropped to his knees.

Grace didn't move, didn't breathe. She searched his face and was stunned by the stark terror she saw.

"...in the heart?" he whispered and fell over onto his back. He lay there for a moment, staring at the ceiling, his chest rising and falling raggedly with no detectable pattern.

Grace glanced at Lonnie as she dropped to her knees beside Bull. "Bull..." But she didn't know what to say to him. Instead, she pleaded with Lonnie. "Don't do this. Please let me get him a doctor."

Lonnie only grinned.

Bull tightened his grip on her arm as he shifted his gaze to her. "Don't leave me…"

Grace was moved—quite unexpectedly—by his desperation and fear. She laid her free hand over Bull's hand on his chest, blood coating his fingers. "Bull, it's going to be all right." She couldn't believe she had any compassion for this man, yet even after everything he'd done to her, she didn't wish death on him. "I'll get a doctor."

He moved his lips as if to answer, but they stilled. His eyes glazed over, and a single, deep breath escaped him.

And he was gone.

Grace watched him for a moment, unsure of her feelings. Bull had slipped into eternity, a place, according to Thad, of fire and brimstone, of unquenchable thirst and unending misery.

Worse. Eternal separation from God.

The thought sent a chill down her spine, and Grace pulled her arm free from her husband. Like the mist of a spring morning, her hate dissipated. Everything he'd done to her all at once didn't seem so awful. Not so bad as to warrant an eternity in Hell. Wishing him dead had been one thing. Watching him slip over into the abyss, another. She believed Bull was now paying for his sins…and she pitied him. She didn't hate him after all.

And she did not want to meet the same fate.

Grace wasn't afraid of dying so much. She simply realized she did not want to be separated from God. She wanted a chance to know Him. *God, I'm sorry I turned my back on You so long ag—*

"Your turn, luv." Grace flinched and slowly rose to her feet, terrified not of Lonnie but of where he could send her. He cocked his head, appraising her. "The only thing is, you're not abused *enough*." He holstered the gun in his vest pocket, crossed the room in two steps, and backhanded Grace. Pain radiated through her face as she spun against the fireplace mantle.

She caught herself and tried to shake the stinging, burning fog from her brain.

If you're ever in a knock-down-drag-out, Greg, fight with everything you've got. Forget the rules. Go for the vulnerable spots on a man.

Grace would have sworn Thad was in the room with her, his voice came to her so clearly. And she didn't hesitate. Lonnie grabbed her shoulder and jerked her back around, his fist reared back and ready to strike again. Grace rammed her knee into his groin with vicious force. He gasped deeply enough to inhale Chicago and doubled over. Grace snatched the gun from his pocket, but Lonnie caught her hand and fought viciously, trying to wrench it from her.

They wrestled and spun, knocking a vase off the piano. He jerked their hands over his head, trying to move the revolver out of her reach, but he wasn't tall enough. She hung on and fought like a crazed Indian. She dug her nails into his hands and stomped his foot with the sharp heel of her boot. She kneed him again, but he blocked her. Sweaty, terrified, her heart careening, Grace twisted, tried to turn the gun—

And it fired.

They both froze. Their eyes locked.

Lonnie's grip slackened and he staggered back,

releasing the gun. She raised it higher, pointing it at his head. A blood stain blossomed on his chest. He looked down, his brow knit with confusion, and touched the blood.

Lonnie growled and shook his head. He came back to Grace, and she saw the hate in him, knew he had fight left. "Lonnie, please don't make me..."

His eyes burned with murder and vengeance. He took a step toward her, raising his hands to attack.

Fight with everything you've got.

Grace squeezed the trigger again. And again. Each time, the gun jumped in her hand and the explosions rang in her ears. She fired twice more. Lonnie stumbled back and collapsed in the doorway.

Grace's finger went on pulling the trigger over and over and over, but the empty gun only clicked. Finally, her arm dropped to her side, and Lonnie's .32 slipped from her fingers.

Chapter Thirty-One

❧

"And you say the SGA took this vote in June?"

Thad nodded at Katie, sitting on the opposite side of his father's desk, but she had her head down, furiously writing notes. "Yes," he said. "I understand there was only one dissenting vote."

Delicate red curls framed her face and caressed her high cheekbones. She was pretty as ever, but he couldn't recall why he'd been so enamored with her. And he'd wanted to marry her?

The heart was a strange beast. Ironically, the two people who had betrayed him and shattered his soul were the two people he missed so much it hurt. He couldn't believe Pa and Grace had only been gone a month. It felt like forever. Yet, he'd gotten over Katie in days.

"Did you miss me at all?"

The question stilled her hand. She heaved a little sigh and lifted her gaze to him. He recalled being hypnotized not all that long ago by those strangely amber eyes. Now, she was just another pretty face. "Thad, I don't want to hurt your feelings. And we've talked about this."

He picked up a pencil and doodled on the notepad in front of him. "I'm just trying to figure some things out, Katie."

"Did you miss *me?*"

For about a week, he had. Then spring round-up, branding, moving the herd, and ranching had eased the pain. "Truth is, I missed having someone around. I missed making plans, but..."

"You didn't miss *me*." She smirked at him, like he knew that, of course. "We weren't meant to be, Thad. You love ranching. I love writing, traveling, and covering stories."

"I reckon," he muttered, sounding as distracted as he felt. He thought of Grace every day, felt like every minute. Shoot, she never left his mind. He longed to go riding with her and show her that butte he wanted to build a home on. Stepping into Pa's shoes and heading up the ranch with Nick and Adam's blessings hadn't dulled the pain of her absence. He didn't understand it.

Katie closed her notebook and huffed an impatient sigh. "I wanted to finish this interview before I gave you something, as I thought it might distract you. I can see now that was a mistake." She shrugged as if resigned to ending the conversation. "There are several other folks I want to interview anyway." She opened the little reticule hanging from her wrist and fished out a yellow piece of paper. A telegram.

"Momma picked this up in town yesterday. It's a week old. She said I was to give it to you."

Thad's stomach did a funny kind of wiggle as he reached across the desk to take the paper from her.

Katie held onto it as he tugged. "She said I was to tell you, and I quote, 'you're burning daylight.'"

Puzzled, Thad tugged again and Katie released the telegram. Oddly positive the note was of great import, he unfolded it, praying it was from Grace.

Dear Raney. Bull has been murdered. I have Hardy. Settling affairs here. Miss you all so much. Will write soon. Love, Grace

Katie stood up and cocked an eyebrow at him. "You're burnin' daylight, cowboy."

***

Grace dropped one last bag just inside the front door and waved at the carriage driver to let him know they were nearly ready. She counted six bags, the total of their belongings. "Hardy, are you ready?" she called up the stairs.

"Coming, Mommy."

"Hurry, please, the cab is waiting." Slipping into her coat, she glanced around the silent house. Pieces of furniture covered in sheets haunted every room like ghosts. The auction was only a few days away now, but she wouldn't be here for it. She and Hardy were leaving with nothing but some clothes and a few toys. Everything was to be sold, and the money given to orphanages and halfway houses. At least some good would come from the man who had damaged so many lives. Perhaps her plans for Bull's estate had convinced the police of her innocence even more than the actual truth. With the investigation closed, she could move on.

Since Grace had not received any response from Raney, or anyone else in Wyoming, she had contacted Susanna Kinsey. The actress seemed genuinely delighted to play hostess. The arrangement would have to do, at least for a while. Grace would visit her grandparents soon, perhaps move back to Pennsylvania. And she still hoped to become a teacher.

Truthfully, she pined for the wide-open spaces and towering mountains of Wyoming. She missed the soothing sound of lowing cattle and the handsome cowboy on his big bay mare. She snatched her gloves from her pockets, annoyed with herself. *Leave that dream on the shelf, Grace.*

A shadow darkened the door and she turned, thinking the driver had come for their bags.

She gasped and stepped back.

Thad stood in the entrance, wearing a thick, sheepskin coat and an impish grin that highlighted his dimple. He snatched his hat off and hugged it to his chest. "Hello, Mrs. Hendrick."

"Thad?" her voice cracked. She cleared her throat and tried again. "Thad. What are you doing here?"

The grin widened. "You owe me five dollars for a telephone call, Buttercup."

Grace's mouth nearly fell open. She fought the smile that threatened to unleash a flood of tears as her heart hammered in her breast. "You came all this way for five dollars?"

Thad stepped up to her and searched her eyes. "I figured somethin' out while you were gone."

Grace swallowed but couldn't speak. His gaze, warm and hopeful, left her incapable.

He lifted a hand to her cheek. "You're the one." He ran his thumb over her lips. "I haven't stopped thinking about you for one second. And knowing what he might be doing to you nearly tore me apart. I kept asking God for some direction, some door to open..." His voice sounded strangled and he stopped for a moment, the muscles in his jaws tightening. "I love you, Grace. There's nothin' holding you here now. Come back to Wyoming with me...as my bride."

Grace barely held back a joyful sob as her knees weakened with sheer exultation. He'd come for her. He'd come all the way to Chicago. "I didn't think you wanted me. I thought you hated me."

Thad slid his arms inside her coat and pulled her to him. He kissed her hungrily, deeply, kissed her until she had no strength in her legs, and she clung to him. "Ah, Grace, I'm so sorry." He kissed her lips, her nose, and her forehead. "I am a special kind of idiot." He hugged her tighter, as if he wanted to mold to her every line and curve. Grace let herself get lost in his arms, in the steel of his chest, in his protection. She felt safe and...complete. Nibbling along her jaw, flirting with her earlobe, he whispered, "Promise me something?"

His hot breath gave her chills. She felt faint with bliss and a hunger for him that frightened her. At that moment, she would have promised him anything. She nodded.

He leaned back so he could look at her, dropping his hands possessively to her waist. She reached up to touch the place in his cheek where the dimple lived, but the intensity in his gaze, the set of his jaw, stayed her hand. He raised one side of his mouth. "Promise me you'll never be anything but a lady."

She raised her right hand. "I promise."

"Mommy?" Hardy's puzzled tone separated Thad and Grace with a jolt. Smiling, she rushed to her son as he ambled cautiously down the stairs.

"Hardy, there's someone here I want you to meet." She took his hand and led him over to Thad. "Thad Walker, this is my son Hardy. Hardy, Thad here is a real cowboy. He and his family own the biggest ranch in Wyoming."

The boy's eyes bugged. Thad squatted down to the four-year-old's level. "Hardy, it sure is nice to meet you." The two shook hands.

"Do you have a bunkhouse?" the child asked, awestruck.

Thad chuckled. "I sure do. A pretty big one."

"Can I see it sometime?"

Thad's grin spread. He flicked his gaze quickly at Grace and rapped his knuckles on Hardy's chest. "See it? Why, I might even let you stay in it sometime."

Hardy's eyes saucered again, even bigger this time.

Laughing, Thad rose to his feet and tried for a serious tone. "Mrs. Hendrick, I'd like to ask again. Is there any possibility you and this fine young man would accompany me back to Wyoming? Hardy, I'm always looking to hire more cowboys."

Perhaps a little overwhelmed, the boy scooted

closer to Grace and took her hand. "I don't know how to be a cowboy."

"Well, if you'd like to learn, your ma here and me, we could teach you."

His mouth forming a little *O*, Hardy stared up at Grace. "You know how to be a cowboy?"

"Thad taught me everything I know."

"And she's not half-bad." Thad punched Grace in the arm. That ridiculous grin made her want to kiss him and slap him at the same time. "What do you say, Mrs. Hendrick?" He gave her a roguish wink. "I need more ranch hands. 'Specially now that we're mergin' with the Diamond R."

She bit her lip and looked down at her son. "What do you say, Hardy? Would you like to see Wyoming? Maybe learn to cowboy?"

Hardy nodded so enthusiastically that his head looked like it was on a rickety swivel. Grace shoved her hand out to Thad. "Well, Mr. Walker...will you take us on? The *both* of us?"

Thad bent down and picked up a bag on each side of Grace, then stood, drawing almost nose-to-nose with her. He pondered her lips and looked into her eyes. "I promised—*swore*, in fact—that I wouldn't cheat Raney out of a wedding. You have no idea how that promise grieves me now."

Grace touched his arm, regretting so much that she couldn't kiss him like she wanted to with Hardy present. But she grinned, and knew he understood all the things she *couldn't* say. "Then take us home, Mr. Walker. We're burnin' daylight."

A Look at *A Lady in Defiance*

ROMANCE IN THE ROCKIES
BOOK ONE

HIS TOWN. HER GOD. LET THE BATTLE BEGIN.

In the mining town of Defiance, Charles McIntyre reigns over everything and everyone, his empire built on ambition and control. When three Christian sisters from the South arrive, stranded and eager to open a hotel, Charles is intrigued—especially by the feisty middle sister, Naomi.

But Naomi, still reeling from the loss of her husband, is furious with God and determined to avoid both Defiance and the saloon-owning man who embodies everything she despises. Yet, as fate would have it, God seems intent on weaving their lives together. The question looms: does God truly have a plan for each and every life?

With a gritty realism that defies the conventions of historical Christian fiction, *A Lady in Defiance* pays homage to classics like *Pride and Prejudice* and *Redeeming Love*. Based on true events, this ensemble narrative intertwines the lives of the three sisters and the rowdy residents of Defiance, exploring love, faith, and the transformative power of grace.

AVAILABLE DECEMBER 2024

About the Author

Heather Blanton is a *USA Today* bestselling author of thirty Christian Western romances, including the highly rated and awarded Romance in the Rockies series. She is also an award-winning script writer.

She grew up in the mountains of Western North Carolina on a steady diet of *Bonanza, Gunsmoke,* and John Wayne Westerns. Her daddy taught her to shoot when she was five, and she can hit that at which she aims.

Her novels are all Christian Western romance because she enjoys creating feisty pioneer women who struggle to find love and hold on to their faith. Like all good, old-fashioned Westerns, there is always justice, a moral message, American values, lots of high adventure, unexpected plot twists, and often a touch of suspense.

www.authorheatherblanton.com